THE CHRISTMAS VILLAGE

by

Melissa Ann Goodwin

ISBN: 1463646259
ISBN-13: 9781463646257
LCCN: 2011911019

Dedication
For my husband, Richard, with love and gratitude.

TABLE OF CONTENTS

CHAPTER 1

The rain just made everything worse. Jamie pressed his nose against the passenger window and peered into the darkness. The car whizzed past house after house decorated with colorful Christmas lights, but on this dismal night, the scene only reminded him of those sidewalk chalk drawings that look blurry and sad after a rainstorm.

It was five days before Christmas, and Jamie Reynolds and his mom were headed to his grandparents' house in Bell's Crossing, Vermont. They had been driving all day through gloomy weather, stopping only for bathroom breaks and a greasy hamburger with soggy fries at a place called Red's Diner. Under ordinary circumstances, Jamie would have been a lot more excited to spend two weeks at Grandma and Grandpa Johnson's. But these weren't ordinary circumstances, not by a long shot.

The overly warm car smelled like stale air and leftover fries. Jamie's eyes had grown weary from reading the book that now lay face-down in his lap. The monotonous *thunk thunk thunk* of the windshield wipers made him drowsy. To amuse himself, Jamie squinted so that the lights whizzed past in a kaleidoscope of streaks and swirls.

Mom said, "Penny for your thoughts."

Jamie slumped deeper into his seat and propped his stocking feet on the dashboard. "Save your money," he muttered, "I'm too tired to think."

It wasn't true, of course. Thoughts ricocheted like pinballs inside his head. Everything seemed to have happened so fast. A few weeks ago, Jamie was just an average seventh grader at Emerson Junior High in Hardcastle, Virginia, playing mid-fielder on the soccer team and hanging out with his friends. Almost overnight, that had all changed. His dad was gone and his mother cried all the time. Everybody talked *about* them, but no one talked *to* them.

Yesterday, Jamie's best friend Tommy dropped the worst bombshell of all. "My parents say I can't hang out with you anymore." Tommy lowered his eyes and dug the toe of his boot into the sidewalk. "I mean, I know it's not your fault ... about what your dad did, I mean. You ... you know what I mean," he stammered. "I'm *really* sorry, Jamie."

Jamie tried to speak, but his mind felt frozen and his throat felt as though it had clamped shut. He shrugged and thrust his hands deep into his pockets, blinking back tears as he watched his best friend in the whole world turn and walk away.

Back home, Jamie bolted up the stairs, his body shaking with sobs. He slammed his bedroom door and hurled himself onto the bed. Mom ran in after him. "What's wrong, Jamie?" she cried. "What's wrong?"

"Everything's wrong!" he screamed through choking sobs. "Just leave me alone!"

Jamie's mom sat on the bed and reached out to stroke his hair. He pushed her hand away and propped himself on his elbow. He swiped his sleeve beneath his runny nose. Salty tears burned his lips as he spat out his words. "Everybody hates us. And it's all Dad's fault! It's not fair! I wish everything could go back to the way it was before. I wish we could go someplace where nobody knows us. Some place where people don't talk behind our backs." Bitterly he added, "Or in front of our faces."

The color drained from Mom's face. "I know it's hard, honey. Believe me I know how hard it is. Your dad made some serious mistakes and a lot of people are angry about what he did. But everybody doesn't hate us. Not *everybody*."

"Name one person," Jamie snarled.

Mom bit her bottom lip and tears pooled in her hazel eyes. "We've got Grandma and Grandpa and Auntie Jess and Uncle Dave —"

"They're family! They don't count!"

"Don't you ever say that!" Mom cried. "Family always counts!"

Jamie hung his head but pressed his lips together and didn't respond.

Mom took a deep breath and touched his shoulder lightly. "Jamie, I know that everything seems confusing right now. It's confusing to me too. Things look bad, but a big part of me still believes in Dad and is hoping that this is all just a huge mistake. No matter what, we still have our family and friends. We still have friends, Jamie, ones that won't desert us. We do."

That morning, Jamie opened his eyes to see his mother standing near his bureau, folding clothes and placing them in a duffle bag. His favorite blue wool sweater from L.L. Bean, a red t-shirt, blue jeans, gym socks and underwear hung neatly over his desk chair. "What's going on?"

Mom gave Jamie a bright smile, though redness rimmed her eyes and dark circles showed beneath them. "*We*," she said, with a lilt in her voice, "are going to Grandma and Grandpa Johnson's house, and *we* are going to spend the holidays with them." She flipped her wavy brown hair behind her shoulders and dropped an armload of rolled-up socks into the duffle bag.

"Today? Now?" Jamie swung his feet over the edge of the bed.

Mom faced him, hands on hips. "Yes. Now. Right now. I just finished that big article about wind power for the magazine, so Mr. Lowenstein said I could take off as much time as I need. And I called the school to let Principal Norman know that you'll be missing a few days. So I want you to shower, and we'll have breakfast, and then we'll get on the road. It's a ten hour drive."

Jamie dressed quickly after showering and inspected himself in the mirror. He used his fingers to comb through his thick brown hair, which had a maddening tendency to stick out around his ears and at the crown of his head. He noticed that his face looked pale in contrast to his brown eyes and straight dark brows. The light freckles that dotted his nose and cheeks seemed to stand out more than usual too. He got the hair and freckles from his mother, but everyone always said that he had his dad's smiling eyes. He made a sour face at himself in the mirror and thought ruefully, *but that was before, when we used to smile.*

Now they had been traveling for eight hours, which to Jamie seemed like a lifetime. It didn't help that he'd slept badly, tossing and turning all last night. He'd had that awful nightmare again – the one where a man was chasing him through a dark, bone-chillingly cold building. He always managed to wake up just as the man was about to catch him. Jamie shivered at the memory.

They passed a sign that read BELL'S CROSSING 120 MILES. *Two more hours to go.* Jamie sighed heavily. It was hard for him to imagine ever going back home and facing their friends and neighbors again. After what his dad had done, after the awful shame of it, how could they go back? No, he just didn't see how it was possible. Anger welled up and clamped hold of Jamie's heart. *It's so unfair!* he thought for the millionth time. *I'll never forgive Dad for ruining our lives. Never.* Jamie yanked on the lever that reclined his seat. His book slid to the floor and landed with a thud. He lay back with his eyes closed and let the hypnotic beat of the wipers drown out his thoughts as he drifted off to sleep.

CHAPTER 2

"Don't come in here!" Grandma called from behind the closed living room doors. "I want this to be a surprise."

"Okay, Grandma, but when are you going to be done, for Pete's sake? You've been in there all morning!" Jamie backed away from the crack between the doors, through which he had been trying to peek.

"Good things are worth the wait."

Jamie sighed. That was the kind of thing Grandma always said. He figured that he would just have to find something to do until she was ready to reveal her big secret. He tugged open the heavy wooden front door and gazed through the storm door glass at the glistening golden fields that stretched to the woods. The world outside seemed perfectly silent and still.

Just as he was about to shut the door and head to the den to watch television, Jamie glimpsed movement where the field met the trees. A graceful doe, almost the same golden shade as the dead winter grass, stepped into the open.

She looked around as though making sure all was safe, then cautiously walked further out. A second later, two fawns appeared behind her. Delighted, Jamie opened the storm door and stepped onto the porch.

The rain had stopped during the night and the sun shone brightly in a clear blue sky. Jamie couldn't even remember driving up to the house last night, or bringing in the luggage, or climbing into the soft bed with the warm quilts and goose down pillows. He'd slept until almost nine o'clock, but Grandma made him a huge breakfast of scrambled eggs, crisp bacon and her famous gooey cinnamon-pecan rolls anyway.

He wrapped his arms around his body and bounced up and down. His breath was like smoke in the crisp air, but the sun felt strong and warm on his face. He watched the fawns frolic in the sunny field while their mother kept a watchful eye. Suddenly the doe stopped and looked toward the house. Jamie froze and held his breath, not wanting to scare her off. She stared at him for what seemed like a long time. Then using her nose, she prodded her babies back toward the woods. A moment later, the three deer disappeared into the trees.

Jamie went back inside and grabbed his navy blue parka from its hook in the mudroom. He slipped out the back door and trudged across the half-frozen, half-muddy field. At the edge of the woods, he climbed onto a mossy stone wall and balanced his way along it. The deer were nowhere to be seen.

After a while Jamie stopped and looked back toward Grandma and Grandpa's house. At this distance it looked as tiny as a doll's house, with a comforting stream of wood smoke rising from the living room chimney. He loved the old place, with its creaky wooden floors and cozy rooms warmed by clanky metal radiators and wood burning fireplaces. It had a wide front porch lined with five old wooden rockers that creaked, and a small red barn that still smelled faintly of the horse and chickens they had once kept there. Now Grandpa used the barn as a workshop where he made benches that he sold in a shop in town.

Jamie inhaled deeply. The air smelled fresh and clean after the rain. It felt good to be outside, and to be here in Bell's Crossing, where no one knew about his dad or what he had done. Looking up at the cloudless sky, Jamie wondered if it would snow in time for Christmas.

He spent the rest of the day wandering around the field, balancing along the wall and throwing rocks into the woods. It was almost suppertime when he pushed the back door open. The warmth of the house and the smells of coffee and freshly-baked biscuits instantly embraced him. He plunked down on one of Grandpa's handmade benches in the mud room and pulled off his boots. Voices drifted from the kitchen.

"It'll just take time," Grandpa said.

"I know," said Grandma, "but it's a shame, that's all. It's not right for a child to have to suffer for what a parent's done."

"True enough. But Jamie's a smart boy. He knows that just because his father did wrong, it's no reflection on Lisa or him."

"I don't know, Bart. Seems to me that Lisa's not doing all that well herself. She puts up a good front for the boy, but she's worn down by this. You know she didn't even get out of bed until noontime, and then she went back to sleep around three."

"Well, a lot of people are mighty angry about what Dale did. The worst part is that they wonder if Lisa knew what he'd been up to. People can be hard when they feel like their trust has been broken."

"Nobody's trust was broken any more than our Lisa's!" Grandma's tone sounded sharp and Jamie heard a cupboard door bang shut a little louder than necessary.

"I just wish that Dale would have come to us for help, but he never did. He just kept everything to himself until it was too late."

Jamie reached over and turned the knob on the back door. He opened it wide and then slammed it shut, as if he'd just come inside. He called out, "Grandma, what's that I smell baking?" He banged his boots on the floor and waited another minute before padding into the kitchen in his stocking feet.

Grandpa held a cup of steaming coffee in one hand and a biscuit in the other. A plate of butter and an open jar of strawberry jam sat on the table in front of him. "C'mon over here and join me in one of Granny's buttermilk biscuits," he said, pulling a chair away from the table. "These things just melt in your mouth."

"Wait, Bart," said Grandma, "there's something I want to show Jamie first." She took Jamie's hand and led him down the hall. "I finished that secret project I was working on this morning." They stopped in front of the living room doors. "Now close your eyes," Grandma ordered.

Jamie obeyed. He heard the doors creak open.

"Okay, now you can look."

The sweet scent of pine floated on the air. A fire roared in the magnificent stone hearth and threw its heat across the room. The mantel was decorated with evergreens and holly. A ten-foot-tall Christmas tree shimmered with tinsel, sparkling glass ornaments and twinkling white lights.

"It's beautiful, Grandma," Jamie said.

"Now over here is the *piece de resistance*," said Grandma, leading him across the room.

"What does that mean?"

"It's a French expression that means, the Star of the Show, the Belle of the Ball, the . . . the . . . the Main Attraction!"

Grandma's Main Attraction was a village of miniature porcelain cottages nestled in a blanket of cotton-batting snow on top of a long table. Perched on a knoll overlooking the village was a white church. Below the church stood a regal pine tree. A group of carolers gathered in a half-circle beneath the tree, their heads thrown back and their mouths open in O's of song.

A sign on a brick building read Canterbury Town Hall and another read Canterbury Post Office. Aunt Polly's Kitchen and The Canterbury Savings Bank rounded out Main Street, which was lined with tiny streetlamps decorated with red bows. A tiny statue of a soldier stood in the town square. Scattered about the village were other buildings: Miss Ida's Boarding House, Vanderzee's Welding & Ironworks and the Canterbury General Store.

On a hill at the outskirts of the village, a blue Victorian mansion with gables and two chimneys overlooked a cluster of cozy cottages. At the very center of the village was a glass pond on which two figures, a boy and girl, skated. Though they were tiny – less than two inches tall – Jamie could make out every detail of their clothing. The girl wore a red coat with matching hat, a white scarf and gloves, red and white striped stockings and white skates. The boy wore a blue jacket with gold buttons, gray pants and hat, and a blue striped scarf and mittens. In a clearing near the pond, a black Scottish terrier with a red plaid bow around its neck sniffed at a snowman that sported a black top hat and a bright orange scarf with a large black "P" on one end.

Jamie put his arm around Grandma's ample hips. "You're right, Grandma. This is definitely a Piece of Resistance. Definitely. I think I remember this village from when we came here for Christmas when I was really small."

"That's right. I used to put it out every Christmas when your mom and your Aunt Jess were children, and those first few years when you were little and everyone came up here for the holidays. But ever since we started coming down to spend holidays with you in Virginia, I haven't had much occasion to put out my decorations. When I was poking around in the attic yesterday, I saw the boxes and decided it was the perfect time to bring the Christmas Village out again."

They admired the village in silence, the snapping of the wood fire and the ticking of the grandfather clock the only sounds in the room. Then Grandma squeezed Jamie's shoulder and said, "Let's go have our dinner, shall we?"

Later that evening, Jamie wandered into the living room for a last look before bed. Crimson embers glowed in the hearth. Grandpa snored loudly but peacefully in his chair. Jamie tiptoed past him to peer at the Christmas Village. He imagined the skaters trudging home, their skates thrown over their shoulders and their cheeks rosy from wind and cold. He pictured the banker closing up for the night and the welders returning to their cozy cottages after a long day at work. He imagined a choir practicing in the church and happy families eating pot roast and biscuits smothered with honey in front of warm fireplaces.

Jamie imagined how perfect life would be in a perfect little village like Canterbury. His heart ached to live in such a place, where nothing ever changed. "I wish I could live in Canterbury," he whispered. Then he tiptoed past his snoring grandpa and quietly closed the doors behind him.

CHAPTER 3

"I wonder which house they live in." Jamie lay on the sofa with his head in his mother's lap. He was close to finishing his book, but his eyelids had begun to droop so he set it aside for tomorrow. Grandma sat knitting in her red brocade armchair to one side of the crackling fire, and Grandpa dozed in his worn leather chair on the other side, his *New Yorker* magazine resting in his lap. The flickering firelight cast a warm glow over their faces. They had been at Grandma and Grandpa's house for two days now, and the awful events of the past few weeks were beginning to slip into the background.

"Who?" Mom asked.

"The boy and girl on the skating pond. Do you think they are friends, or brother and sister?"

Mom hesitated, then played along. "Oh! You mean Kelly and Christopher! They're brother and sister. He's twelve years old like you, and Kelly is ten. They live in that big house up on the hill – the blue Victorian with the fancy porch and gingerbread trim."

Jamie cocked his head as if to say, *Yeah, right, Mom.* Ignoring his expression, she continued. "Now, you see that place over there? The white house with the red roof and the cupola on top? That's Miss Ida's Boarding House. Miss Ida is a widow – her husband died in the First World War. She runs the boarding house to make ends meet."

"What does she look like?"

"Oh, Miss Ida is as plump as a ripe pumpkin! She has fiery red hair and green eyes that twinkle. And freckles. *Hundreds* of freckles. Miss Ida loves to cook, and she loves to eat what she cooks. She won the pie contest at the Canterbury Summer Festival three years running. She makes chicken pot pie and chicken with dumplings and apple pie that melts in your mouth. She wears a red-checkered apron over her dress, and her cheeks are always flushed from working near a hot stove. Miss Ida is very kind and she'll take anyone in if she thinks they've fallen on hard times."

"How does she make any money then?"

"Sometimes people trade work for room and board. One fellow chops and hauls wood and another feeds the chickens and milks the cow. Some will do handyman work, like fixing a busted floorboard on the porch or patching leaks in the roof. Things like that."

"The people are dressed kind of old-fashioned," Jamie said.

"That's because the year is 1932. It's the Great Depression. You know what that is, right?"

Jamie nodded. "We learned about it in school. It's after the stock market crashed and people lost all their money and couldn't find jobs."

"That's right. In fact, you see Vanderzee's over there? Before the Depression started, that place was going day and night. Now it's closed and most of the men have had to go to other towns to find work."

Jamie said, "But the boy and girl, Kelly and Christopher, they look kind of rich, don't they?"

"Yes, some people who didn't have their money in stocks did all right. Their father, Mr. Pennysworth, runs the bank – the Canterbury Savings Bank there on Main Street."

"That's funny! The banker's name is *Pennys*worth!" Jamie pointed to the smallest cottage. "Who lives over there, in the little white cottage with the gray roof?"

"That's Mrs. Gordon's house. She lives there with her baby Emilie."

"Where is Mr. Gordon?"

A shadow crossed Mom's face and she paused before answering. "He's one of the men who lost his job and had to look for work somewhere else."

Jamie was about to ask if Mr. Gordon was coming back, but he stopped himself. Ever since he was small, Mom had always made up wonderful stories for him. For a few minutes, she had made Canterbury and the people in it sound so real that he had almost forgotten that she was doing it again. He gazed for a long time at the peaceful village. The smells of Christmas filled the room, the piney aroma of the tree, the wood fire, the scent of an apple-cranberry candle burning on the coffee table. Jamie closed his eyes and made his wish again: *I wish I could live in Canterbury. I wish, I wish, I wish.*

CHAPTER 4

The next morning Jamie and Mom went into town for groceries. Bell's Crossing buzzed with the electric energy of people hurrying to do their last minute Christmas shopping. In spite of the fact that parking spaces were scarce and the stores were crowded, people were in the holiday spirit, smiling and calling out greetings across the busy street.

Jamie loved the Bell's Crossing General Store, with its wide pine floorboards that creaked and bounced a little underfoot. An ancient mustiness lingered beneath the fresh scent of lemony floor polish. Each aisle held surprises, like packages of iced Petit Fours nestled on the shelf beside jars of pickled herring. At the General Store, you could buy groceries, a pair of warm wool socks, a wrench, a toboggan, a stepladder or a frying pan.

Mom gave Jamie the shopping list and let him push the cart while she went in search of a muffin pan that Grandma needed. Petit Fours weren't on the list, but the picture of thinly-sliced cake layered with jam and frosting made Jamie's mouth water, so he slid a box of them into the cart.

As he rounded the aisle near the register, two women at the checkout counter blocked his way. The taller one had stiffly-sprayed, orangey-red hair. She wore tight black stretch pants that squished her large bottom into an odd assortment of lumps and bulges. The woman whispered loudly, "That's Bart and Esther's girl, Lisa."

"*Ooohhhhh*," replied the friend, a short, skinny woman with closely-cropped black hair and a pinched face. "She's the one who's husband ...."

Red-hair elbowed her friend, winked and said, "*Right*. I heard that he ...." She cupped her hand around her mouth and whispered the rest in her friend's ear.

A scarlet flush crept up Jamie's neck and spread across his face. His cheeks burned and began to throb. His heart raced. His mouth felt as dry as sandpaper. He clenched the bar of the shopping cart so hard that his knuckles turned white. The room spun away from him, and it seemed like his iron-clad grip on the cart was the only thing that kept him from spinning away with it.

Through his daze, Jamie heard the man behind the counter talking. "All right, Lydia, your total comes to $35.62. Is there anything else you need today?" The man's calm voice eased Jamie's mind back down to earth. The spinning slowed and his eyes began to focus. The man had a pleasant face, light brown hair and green eyes that twinkled. He caught Jamie's eye and winked. The women paid, gathered their bundles and headed for the door.

CHAPTER 4

"Hello, son, I'm Sean O'Neill. You must be Bart and Esther's grandson." Without waiting for Jamie's reply, Mr. O'Neill asked, "Is your mom here with you?"

"Ye – yes," Jamie stammered, surprised that he could speak. "She's here somewhere." He whipped his head left and right, his eyes searching for her.

Mr. O'Neill closed the register drawer, lifted a hinged portion of the wooden counter and stepped from behind it. He squatted down until his gaze was level with Jamie's and put his hand on the boy's shoulder. "What's your name, son?"

"Jamie Reynolds, sir."

"Well, Jamie. Don't you be thinking what you're thinking."

Jamie's eyebrows shot up in surprise. How could Mr. O'Neill possibly know what he was thinking?

"You're thinking that you came here to escape your troubles, but they've found you again. Am I right?"

Jamie nodded. A tear trickled down his cheek and landed on his upper lip. Embarrassed, he licked it away with a dart of his tongue.

"Well you're wrong son. Sure, some people like to talk. But most of the people here in Bell's Crossing are good-hearted. And those that aren't, well, their opinions don't much matter anyway. You and your mom are welcome here, and no one will treat you any different. At least not in *my* store. Okay?"

Just then, Mom spotted them and came over. Mr. O'Neill stood and held out his hand. "You must be Jamie's mom. I'm Sean O'Neill. I own the store."

"Lisa Reynolds. Nice to meet you." Her eyes searched Sean and Jamie's faces. "Is everything okay here?"

"Everything is just fine here, Ma'am. Is there anything else I can help you find?"

Jamie pushed the cart behind his mother as they finished gathering the items on the list. When Mr. O'Neill rang up the order, Mom spotted the box of Petit Fours. "Those weren't on the list," she said, pretending to be annoyed.

Jamie looked sheepish. "I know Mom, but they look *sooooo* good. I thought Grandma would like them."

Sean and Lisa laughed. "you thought your grandma would like them, eh, son? Well, I'll bet you're right. And if you're lucky, maybe she'll share them with you."

During the drive home, Jamie stared out the window, lost in thought about what those women had said, about his father, and about how much he wished that everything could just go back to the way it had been before. At last Mom broke the silence. "Mr. O'Neill seemed like a nice man."

Jamie slouched far down in his seat. "Yep."

"Did something happen in the store?"

"I don't want to talk about it." Jamie crossed his arms tightly over his chest and stared out the window. The sky had turned gray and overcast again. Dark storm clouds gathered in the distance.

Mom sighed. "Okay. But if you decide you want to talk, I'm here to listen." They drove the rest of the way home in silence.

CHAPTER 5

*B*ong ... *Bong* ... *Bong* ....
    Jamie stirred from a deep sleep. *The church*, he thought dreamily, *the church bells are chiming*. He bolted upright.

Bong.

His brain felt foggy. He wasn't in his bed. This wasn't his house. *Where am I?*

Bong.

Oh! He remembered now. He was at Grandma and Grandpa's house. He was lying on the living room couch, covered with one of Grandma's colorful patchwork quilts. The fire had burned down to embers and the air smelled of charred pine. The full moon peeked between the curtains and beamed one slender ray of light across the floor.

Bong.

He finally realized that it was the grandfather clock over by the living room doors that was chiming.

Bong.

How many was that?

Bong.

Jamie peered at the clock and vaguely made out the hands pointing straight up.

Bong.

Still groggy, he realized that he must have fallen asleep on the couch. He'd had a bad day and it had exhausted him. Hearing those women talking in the General Store had put him in a foul mood. After he got home, Jamie had moped around his room until suppertime. Guiltily, he remembered snapping at his mother and doing little more than grunting at his grandparents while barely tasting the hearty beef stew that Grandma had labored over all day.

Bong.

Later, he'd come into the living room, hoping to regain some of the good feelings that had disappeared at the store. The last thing he remembered was sinking into the plush forest-green velvet cushions of the couch and escaping into the final chapters of his book.

Bong.

Jamie noticed that he still had on the dark blue corduroy pants and red and green flannel shirt he'd worn all day. He realized that his mother probably hadn't had the heart to wake him up, so she must have covered him with the quilt and let him sleep on the couch. He felt even guiltier knowing that she had taken care of him even though he had been in such a surly mood.

Bong.

CHAPTER 5

Midnight. Jamie hadn't been awake at midnight since the time he slept over at Tommy's and they had tried to stay awake all night by telling ghosts stories and making scary faces over the flashlight.

Suddenly Jamie heard whispers. He froze, listening hard. There they were again! His heart beat faster. Was there someone else in the room?

He heard laughter – a girl's laughter. The hair on the back of his neck prickled. His eyes searched the room, but he saw no one. More laughter, this time a boy's. Jamie pulled the quilt aside and placed his stocking feet on the worn Oriental rug. *Maybe Grandma and Grandpa's house has ghosts.*

The sounds seemed to come from the direction of the Christmas Village. Jamie tiptoed toward the table, his way lit only by the twinkling lights from the Christmas tree. He studied the scene laid out before him, with its tiny cottages nestled in the snow. Something seemed different, but he couldn't quite put his finger on what it was. Then he heard the voices again, much louder this time.

"Christopher! If you do that again, I'll … I'll … I'll!"

"You'll what? Tell on me? Tattletale, tattletale, Kelly is a tattletale!"

Jamie's jaw dropped and his eyes bulged. He knelt down and brought his face level with the top of the table. The girl skater sat on the ice, her tiny red and white striped legs and white skates protruding beneath her tangled red skirt. The boy skated around her, skidded to a stop and extended a hand. The girl grabbed it and pulled herself to her feet. She brushed bits of snow and ice off her skirt. Shaking a white-gloved finger at the boy, she scolded, "I'll get even with you, Christopher Franklin Pennysworth, if it's the last thing I do!"

The boy laughed and skated away. "You'll have to catch me first!" He took two smooth strides and launched into an impressive double axle that carried him halfway across the pond.

Kelly leaned in and sped after him, her arms swinging from side to side with the aggressiveness of an angry hockey player. Christopher paused to let her catch up. Then, when she was just inches away, he peeled off again. She chased him, huffing and puffing and grabbing at his jacket, never quite able to catch up.

Jamie realized that he was holding his breath. It occurred to him that if he reached out, he could pick up the pocket-sized Kelly and Christopher with his fingers, dangling them like King Kong did in the movies. But he didn't dare, because something told him not to cross the invisible boundary that separated his world from theirs. So Jamie stayed perfectly still, barely even breathing, afraid that if he moved or made a sound, he would break what seemed to be a spell that had made the village of Canterbury magically come to life.

CHAPTER 6

Movement at the far corner of the table caught Jamie's eye. He crawled along the floor until he knelt in front of Miss Ida's Boarding House. A man with a bushy red beard carried an armload of firewood across the front porch. He struggled to free a hand so that he could turn the doorknob, then kicked the door wide and stomped inside.

Jamie peered through the frosted windowpanes and watched as the man placed the logs on a brick hearth beside a roaring fire. Although the windows were smaller than his pinky fingernail, Jamie could see inside just as clearly as if he were looking through the windows of Grandma's house.

Six men sat on picnic style benches at a long wooden table in the center of the room. All had full bushy beards of various colors and lengths, and all were slurping soup from large bowls. The man with the red beard squeezed between two other men and ladled soup from a steaming pot into his own bowl. Jamie thought he could actually smell the beef barley soup and freshly-baked bread on their table.

In the kitchen, Miss Ida rolled dough with a wooden rolling pin. Her plump freckled hands stretched out the dough and laid it over a pie plate. She ladled filling into the crust and placed a second crust on top. She wiped her hands on her red-checked apron and said, "This apple pie will be done in one hour, gents. Them what's done their chores is sure to get a piece. Them what hasn't, well, I don't think we'll have to answer that question, now, will we?"

The man with the red beard said, "No, Ma'am, I reckon not." He wiped his hands on a napkin, stood up, and let out a belch loud enough for the neighbors to hear. "Compliments to the chef!" he shouted. The rest of the men roared with laughter.

"Rusty!" Ida turned to face the man, hands on hips. "Mind your manners!"

A man with a long gray beard spoke. "Can't blame him Ida. This soup of yours is fit for a king."

Ida sniffed and turned back to her pie. "Well you boys sure don't act like kings, or even princes, that's for sure."

Rusty wriggled from between his mates on the bench and headed for the kitchen. "I'm on clean-up tonight, so line up your dishes here to my left," he called to the others. He rolled up the sleeves of his red plaid work shirt and began washing pots and pans in the farmhouse style sink. One by one the men finished their soup, rose, and delivered their dishes to be washed. Then they each went off in different directions, presumably to do the chores that would later earn them pie.

CHAPTER 6

"Hey! That hurt!" Jamie's head swiveled toward the pond, where he saw Kelly and Christopher engaged in an all-out snowball fight. He slid back across the floor for a closer look.

Kelly furiously scooped up snow and formed it into a snowball that she lobbed at Christopher's head. He ducked in the nick of time and skated away, laughing. "You missed me, you missed me," he taunted in a sing-song voice.

Kelly raced after him, her blades spitting ice chips. Christopher braked to a stop and scrambled to make another snowball. He pitched it side-arm and caught Kelly on the sleeve. Then he raced off again, with Kelly in hot pursuit.

Crrrraaak! Kelly skidded to a stop. "What was that?" she yelled. *CRRRAAAACK!* A crevice formed in the ice beneath Kelly's feet. A heartbeat later, thousands of small cracks zigzagged outward like shattering glass, until Kelly looked like a fly standing in the center of a spider's web. "Christopher!" she cried, "The ice is breaking!"

On the far side of the pond, Christopher turned just as the ice beneath Kelly's feet caved.

"Help me, Christopher, help me!" she shrieked.

Jamie watched with horror as the ice gave way and Kelly plummeted feet first into the pond.

Christopher raced across the ice. "Kelly! Kelly! Help us someone! Please help us!" he yelled, his voice shrill and shaky. Kelly's head popped up in the water. She thrashed around, trying to swim to the edge of the hole. She tried to crawl onto the ice, but her weight just made more ice break away. She disappeared underwater again.

Christopher lay flat on his stomach, his arm outstretched so that Kelly could grab his hand when she resurfaced. She popped up, gasping for breath. "Take my hand!" Christopher shouted. Kelly reached for it, but he was too far away. She went under for the third time.

Jamie couldn't believe his eyes. His heart pounded and his mind raced. *I've got to do something! I've got to help. If I don't do something, she'll drown!*

Kelly came up once more, her white-gloved hand stretched toward the sky as though she were reaching for someone – any-one – to grab hold of it and pull her out. Without thinking, Jamie reached his own hand across the table, and with his thumb and index finger he grasped Kelly's tiny up-stretched hand.

WHOOOOOSH! The moment Jamie's hand touched Kelly's, he catapulted into a swirling vortex that pulled him down, down, down, his arm outstretched and his hand clamped in the steely grip of an invisible force. His body felt as powerless as a flimsy paperclip being sucked toward a powerful magnet.

Suddenly he plunged head first into ice-cold water. Within seconds, his clothes were soaked through to his skin. Artic cold stung him like a thousand pin pricks and putrid water filled his nostrils. Deeper and deeper he plummeted. Slimy reeds grabbed at his legs. The pressure in his chest felt as though it would crush his lungs.

At last his descent began to slow. He tried to wriggle free, but whatever gripped his hand held it like a vise. Summoning his courage, Jamie opened his eyes. To his astonishment, a pair of terrified blue eyes in a ghostly pale face stared back at him. Long blond hair floated out in every direction, like pictures he had seen of mermaids under the sea. With shock and amazement, Jamie realized that he was looking into the eyes of Kelly Pennysworth, whose pretty face was turning blue, and whose white-gloved hand clutched his own for dear life.

CHAPTER 7

Jamie's throat and lungs burned as though he had swallowed dry ice. He knew he needed to get air – and fast. He signaled thumbs-up, wordlessly letting Kelly know that they needed to swim toward the surface. Gripping each others' hands, they kicked hard and shot upward.

Up, up, up they rose, murky water engulfing them like a ghoulish fog. Jamie kicked with everything he had. *Where's the light? Where's the light?* The words pounded in his brain.

At last he glimpsed a flicker overhead. *Thank heavens!* Jamie squeezed Kelly's hand for encouragement. Hope fueled him as he kicked even harder, until at last they burst through the surface, gagging on bitter pond water and gulping for oxygen.

The cold air pricked his wet face like thumbtacks. He looped an arm around Kelly's shoulders and side-stroked toward Christopher, who still lay on his belly on the ice. "I'm going to try to lift her up to you, okay?"

Christopher's eyes bulged. "Wh – wh – where did you come from? I didn't even see you go into the water!"

"Never mind that now! Just grab hold of her!" Jamie shouted.

"Yes, yes, all right!"

Jamie told Kelly, "I'm going to lift you up and Christopher will pull you out." She nodded. Her eyelashes had clumped into tiny icicles and her teeth chattered.

Furiously treading water, Jamie put his arms around Kelly's hips. He said, "On three then. One. Two. Three!" and hoisted her up. Her water-logged clothes and skates weighed her down so that only her head and shoulders cleared the ice. Christopher stretched his arm toward her, but her fingertips were still just beyond his reach.

Jamie realized that he needed to get Kelly further out onto the ice. He gulped a mouthful of air and dove underwater again. He wrapped his arms around her legs and shoved her upward with all his might. This time, her body lifted up and out of the water as if she had wings.

He surfaced again, gasping for air.

Christopher shouted, "I've got her!"

Jamie treaded water again as he watched Christopher skate backward, dragging Kelly by her arms. He grabbed hold of the jagged edge of the ice and tried to haul himself out, but his arms felt stiff and heavy. He could barely feel his legs and feet. His mind felt numb and all he wanted to do was sleep. His grip on the ice slipped, jolting him momentarily back to consciousness. "Help me! Please help me!" he called, but his voice came out a weak croak.

CHAPTER 7

"Grab hold of this rope, son!" a deep voice boomed. Jamie squinted through frozen eyelashes. He saw Rusty, the red-bearded man from Miss Ida's, lying on his belly on the ice about twenty feet away. Rusty tied a large loop in one end of a rope and tossed it toward Jamie. The rope skidded and danced across the ice, landing just within his reach.

Jamie grabbed the loop and slipped it over his head. Using his last ounce of strength, he raised his arms one at a time to anchor the rope under his armpits.

"Just hang on now, son, I'll pull you out!"

The rope jerked, yanking Jamie up and out of the water like a leaping dolphin. He landed with a thud and his head banged hard against the ice. Weak and stunned, he tried to crawl onto his knees.

Rusty yelled, "Stay down, son, I'll haul you in the rest of the way." Jamie slumped to the ice. *Sleep*, he thought fuzzily. *I just want to sleep.*

The rope dug into his armpits and Jamie felt his body glide across the ice like a human toboggan. His head whacked the ice two or three more times as he bounced along. On the brink of unconsciousness, he glimpsed a small crowd gathered at the edge of the pond. Jamie's last thought before darkness engulfed him was, *Mom is going to kill me for this.*

CHAPTER 8

"H̲e's waking up! He's trying to say something!"
"Ssshhh! Don't startle him. Let him come out of it on his own."

Strange images, scattered memories and confusing thoughts floated to the surface of Jamie's mind like flotsam from a sunken ship. *I had a dream,* he thought, groggily. *A really weird dream.*

He tried to open his eyes, but his eyelids felt like they had been glued shut. He remembered that he had been very cold, but now he felt warm. He managed to open his eyes just enough to see that he lay in a bed covered with thick, colorful patchwork quilts. He made out seven blurry figures standing around his bed. They all had thick bushy beards and all of them looked very worried.

"Where am I? Who are you?" His lips formed the words, but his throat felt parched and his tongue felt fuzzy and thick. His voice came out less than a whisper.

A woman wearing a red and white checked apron pushed between two of the men. As she neared, Jamie detected the sweet scents of vanilla and nutmeg. She took his hand and patted it reassuringly. "There, there, dear," she said, "don't strain yourself."

Jamie stared at the woman's plump, dimpled hand and saw that it was covered with reddish-brown freckles. He lifted his gaze. His eyes widened as he studied her round, freckled face and her sparkling green eyes. He whispered, "I know you. I know who you are."

The red-haired woman threw back her head and laughed. "Of course you do, dearie. I'm Snow White, and these here are none other than my famous Seven Dwarves of which you've heard tell."

The burly, bearded men hooted with laughter and slapped each other's backs. "That's a good one, Ida," said a giant of a man whose jet black beard hung almost down to his belt.

Although his body felt warm, Jamie's mind still felt frozen. He knew where he was, and yet it simply wasn't possible! He really hadn't had time to think before he reached out to pluck Kelly Pennysworth from the pond; he had just known that he had to do something to try to save her. But if he *had* thought about it, he would have imagined picking her up between his thumb and index finger and gently placing her down in the snow by the side of the pond. Never in a million years would it have occurred to him that he would be catapulted out of Grandma and Grandpa's living room and into the miniature village of Canterbury. *Now I've* really *done it,* he thought.

"What's your name, son?" asked Ida.

Jamie whispered through cracked lips, "Jamie."

"Where are you from, Jamie?" asked Rusty.

Jamie wanted to laugh and cry at the same time, because the man's simple question had no simple answer. Did he live in Bell's Crossing now? Or was Hardcastle still his home? How could he tell these people that he came from the living room of Grandma and Grandpa's house, where they all "lived" in tiny cottages that sat on top of a table at Christmastime? How could he tell them that none of them could possibly be real, and that home, as best as he could figure it, lay just beyond the pond from which they had rescued him?

Jamie looked from face to face. "I – I – I ... don't know."

The men exchanged concerned looks. "Sounds like the boy's got that there ambrosia," said one.

"I think you mean amnesia, Fred," said another.

"You mean 'Dopey,' don't you Roy?" joked Rusty.

Fred crossed his arms and glared at Rusty. "Well I – I – I guess that makes you Grumpy, then!" he blurted.

Ida clapped her hands and said, "Now stop that, boys! This is no time for Tom-foolery." She lightly stroked Jamie's hair the way his mom often tried to. Jamie felt too weak to stop her, and besides, it felt nice. Suddenly sorrow overwhelmed him. How many times had he brushed his mother's hand aside when she tried to comfort him? And what was she doing right now? Did she even know that he was gone? Was she already frantic with worry? Tears filled his eyes as waves of guilt, fear and homesickness flooded his heart.

Ida patted Jamie's hand. "There, there. Don't you worry none. You've had some bumps and been slightly frozen, is all. But you're safe and warm here. We'll take good care of you, and in a few days I'm sure you'll be up 'n at 'em, and remember everything there is to be remembered. In the meantime, I'll ask Officer Leahy to start makin' calls around the county to see if he can find your kin. I'm sure they're worried sick and lookin' for you."

Jamie nodded weakly. He watched Ida usher the men out of the room, but her voice sounded a thousand miles away. "We'll take turns stayin' with him, in case he wakes up scared or hungry. Rusty, you stay with him tonight, and the rest of you boys get back to your own business."

"That's dwarves to you, Mistress White," said a deep voice.

"Oh, right! Skedaddle then, dwarves. Snow White has work to do."

"Hey, Harry! I'll bet you a nickel you can't name all seven dwarves," said Roy.

Harry said, "Sure, I can do that. You've got your Dopey and your Grumpy ... your Flopsy, Mopsy and Cottontail ...."

"That's only five."

"Oh yeah. And Donner and Blitzen."

The last thing Jamie heard before drifting off to sleep was the sound of the men chuckling softly as they closed the bedroom door behind them.

CHAPTER 9

Jamie tossed and turned. He was having that dream again, the one where a man was chasing him through a dark, creepy building.

Where is he? Where is he? Jamie crouched beside a large machine in a cavernous, pitch-black room that echoed like the hull of an abandoned ship. Cold air brushed the back of his neck like a ghost's breath. He hugged himself tightly, trying to stop the shivers taking over his body.

The sound of heavy footsteps ricocheted around him. Jamie's head swiveled left and right, his eyes searching the inky darkness. Jamie could not see him, but the gray puffs the man's breath made in the raw damp air betrayed his location. Instinctively, Jamie covered his own mouth with his hand. His eyes darted this way and that, frantically looking for a window or door through which he could escape.

The footsteps stopped. "I know you're in here, boy." An unmistakable hint of malice hovered under the man's words.

Jamie took a deep breath and started to run. Footsteps pounded behind him. Jamie slipped, but recovered quickly. Suddenly the man grabbed the collar of Jamie's coat and yanked it with a force that took Jamie's feet out from under him and sent him sprawling on the floor. Jamie looked up, but all he could see were even white teeth stretched into a sneering, sinister grin that seemed to be floating in empty space, like the Cheshire Cat from Alice in Wonderland.

"I've got you now," the man growled triumphantly.

Thinking fast, Jamie wriggled out of his jacket, scrambled to his feet, and ran. He dove under a machine, rolled to the other side and kept rolling. Then he got up and sprinted. Suddenly his outstretched hands touched rough wood. *The wall!* Jamie side-stepped now, feeling his way across splintery boards. He touched something metal. *A door latch!*

Jamie's hands shook as he yanked the latch up and down. Nothing happened. He tried again. *Please let it open, please.* Trembling all over, he jiggled the latch and shoved hard against the door. Nothing. *Come on!* Jamie's heartbeat pounded in his ears like a drum roll. From the corner of his eye, he glimpsed a shadowy figure darting between machines just a few feet away. The man was so close now that Jamie could almost feel his panting breath.

Jamie's fingers brushed metal again. A slide lock! He fumbled with it and tugged hard. The lock slid an inch and then caught. Wild with panic, he jerked it again. *Please! Please! Please!* his mind screamed. He tugged again, and this time the locking bar slid free.

CHAPTER 9

Jamie threw his weight against the door. It budged an inch, then stuck. *COME ON!* He shoved again. The door budged another inch. *One more time. Make it a good one!* He took a deep breath, leaned back, and rammed the door with all his might.

The rusty old hinges burst off, flinging Jamie through the doorway and face-first into a snow bank. He spat out a mouthful of snow, stood up and ran. In the dim moonlight he saw Ida's Boarding House a hundred yards away. A soft glow shone through the windows and a comforting stream of smoke wafted from the chimney.

Glancing back, Jamie saw his pursuer silhouetted in the doorway. A sign hanging above the door creaked as it swung in the wind. It read "Vanderzee's Welding & Ironworks".

"Run, Jamie, run!" The words echoed in his head but it wasn't his own voice, it was Kelly Pennysworth's voice. "Run, Jamie! Run!" He tried to run but his legs felt stiff and trapped, as though his feet were tied together....

Jamie bolted upright in bed, his heart pounding and his legs flailing beneath the covers, Kelly's voice still ringing in his ears. A sliver of moon cast bluish light through the bedroom window. For a moment, Jamie didn't know where he was. Then he saw Rusty sleeping soundly in an overstuffed armchair in the corner, his feet propped on an ottoman and his red-bearded chin resting on his chest. He made sputtering sounds every time he exhaled. Jamie's heart sank. He'd been dreaming all right, but being in Canterbury was definitely for real.

He lifted the quilts and lowered his feet to the floor. His legs felt wobbly. He saw that he was wearing a man's red flannel nightshirt that was about five sizes too big. He shuffled to the window and looked out.

Deep purple shadows fell across the snow. A hundred yards away, Vanderzee's loomed like a giant tombstone in a snowy graveyard. Leafless vines enshrouded its cold stone walls. Wide boards had been nailed helter-skelter across blank, unseeing windows, as if whoever did it had been in a hurry to finish the job. A battered weathervane twirled mournfully atop a cupola that was missing half its slate shingles. *Why have I been dreaming about being inside Vanderzee's, even before I ever got here? And who was chasing me?*

Rusty snorted and shifted in his chair. Jamie tiptoed past him and cracked open the door. He slipped into the hall and headed toward the window at the other end. From there he could see all the way to the pond. Large tree branches had been laid around the hole in the ice to keep anyone else from falling in.

Jamie puzzled over what had happened to him. *How did I get here? And how will I ever get home? What if I* never *get home? What if I never see Mom or Grandma and Grandpa again?* He blinked back tears.

He tiptoed back down the hallway and eased past the bedroom door. He climbed into bed and pulled the quilts over his head. *I guess I got what I asked for. I wished that I could live in Canterbury and here I am.* Jamie buried his face in his pillow and let his tears flow freely. *I want to go home. I want to get home in time for Christmas. Somehow I got here, and I now I have to find a way to get home. I* have *to.*

CHAPTER 10

Jamie was already awake and sitting up in bed when Ida pushed the bedroom door open the next morning. She carried a tray laden with plates of scrambled eggs, bacon and toast, a glass of orange juice and a mug of steaming hot cocoa. Jamie's stomach responded to the wonderful smells with a loud growl. The last thing he remembered eating was Grandma's stew, and that seemed like an awfully long time ago.

"Rise 'n shine, boys!" Ida sounded as cheerful as a sparrow on a spring morning.

Rusty stirred in his chair. "Mornin' Ida," he said, stretching his arms wide and yawning.

Jamie plumped his pillows and sat up straighter so that Ida could lay the tray on his lap. "How'd you sleep, son?" she asked.

"I slept okay, but I had some strange dreams."

"Well I expect that's normal after what you've been through." Ida turned to Rusty. "How 'bout you, Rusty? You sleep all right in that chair?"

Rusty stretched his long legs and stood up. "I slept just fine. In fact, it was nice not having to listen to the other fellas snore all night."

Jamie loaded his fork with eggs and bacon and gulped them down. "Thank you Miss Ida, this is delicious!"

"You're welcome, son."

"Can I ask you a question, Miss Ida?"

"Sure thing. Ask away."

"What year is it?"

"1932."

"Is today Christmas Eve?"

"What makes you think it's Christmas Eve?"

"Because when I left, it was the day before Christmas Eve."

Ida and Rusty exchanged glances. "When you left where?" Rusty asked.

Jamie realized his mistake and took another bite of food to give himself time to come up with a good answer. He furrowed his brows and pursed his lips as though he was thinking very hard. "I don't know," he finally said, "I just woke up with the idea that today should be Christmas Eve. I guess I'm just confused."

"Well, it's only December the twenty-first. We've got a few days to go until Christmas," Ida said.

Jamie weighed this new information. Apparently, his trip into the Christmas Village had not only taken him back to the year 1932, it had also taken him back to several days before Christmas, instead of Christmas Eve. That fact, as odd as it was, lifted his heart.

"Then I still have time to get home for Christmas – wherever home is."

Ida smiled and squeezed his shoulder. "That's right Jamie, I'm sure we'll have everythin' all figured out before then. Now you eat up, because Doc Fernald is comin' by this mornin' to check you over and I don't want him to accuse me of starvin' you! Would you like a second helpin'?"

"Yes, Ma'am!" Suddenly Jamie felt a lot better about things. He didn't know yet how he would get home by Christmas, but at least he had time to figure it out.

"I do believe that I see a bit of color in those cheeks of yours," said Ida. She felt his forehead with the back of her plump, freckled hand. "No fever." Her face softened. "Now you just rest here until Doc Fernald comes, y'hear?"

"Can I watch tele – ..." Jamie started, then caught himself. He bit his bottom lip. *Darn*, he thought, *there I go again.*

Rusty furrowed his brow. "Watch what, son?"

"Um ... nothing. I just got confused for a minute. Do you have something I could read?"

"I'll bring you the newspaper," Rusty said, and headed out the door.

Jamie didn't usually read the paper at home, but now he was fascinated with every word. The church was having a food and toy collection to help poor families. The Canterbury Quilting Club was meeting on Tuesday at three p.m. in the church hall. The general store advertised specials on cranberries and corned beef hash. There was a notice for a lost gray and white kitten named Bella Luna. Ads offered services such as wood chopping, delivery and handyman chores.

By ten o'clock, Jamie felt as fidgety as a mouse in a house full of cats. He was just thinking about getting out of bed when the door opened and Ida peeked in. "Oh good, you're awake," she said. "Doc Fernald is here to see you."

A tall, thin man with uncombed grayish-brown hair followed Ida into the room. He had a long, pale face lined with deep creases, and wore silver-rimmed glasses with thick lenses. Spiky gray stubble dotted his chin and cheeks. He wore a red plaid bow tie and a threadbare gray wool suit that overwhelmed his thin frame. He carried a cracked and worn black leather satchel. "Hello, son," he said. "I'm Doc Fernald." The doctor smiled, instantly transforming his expression from weary to kind and caring.

"Pleased to meet you, sir."

The doctor sat on the edge of the bed. "I'm just going to give you a little checking over, son. That all right with you?"

"Yes sir. But I feel fine now."

Doc Fernald held his index finger in front of Jamie's nose. "Now follow my finger with your eyes." He moved his finger to the left and then to the right. Next, he pressed his fingers gently on Jamie's throat, just beneath his jaw. He checked the bump on Jamie's head. He listened to Jamie's heart through a stethoscope. Then he held the instrument to Jamie's back and asked him to cough. Doc said, "So, word has it that you're a real true-to-life hero, young man."

Jamie blushed. "I don't know about that, sir."

"Well, I spent half the night and some of the morning up at the Pennysworth place, and I know that they sure as heck think you're a hero."

"How is Kelly?"

Doc stuck a thermometer under Jamie's tongue. "She was very weak when they got her home last night. Her temperature had dropped mighty low. We had to put her in a hot bath and then wrap her in quilts and keep her close to the fire all night."

He removed the thermometer and read the result out loud. "Ninety-eight point five. That's pretty good for taking a swim in arctic waters in late December, I'd say." He shook the thermometer, wiped it clean and put it in his bag. "When I left there this morning, Kelly was awake and feeling hungry. She's going to be just fine."

Doc looked from Jamie to Ida, slapped his hands on his thighs, and said, "Well, I'm afraid that I'm going to have to declare this young man alive and well! Keep feeding him hot, hearty foods, lots of soup and bread and some meat if you've got it."

"Do I have to stay in bed?" Jamie's eyes searched Doc Fernald's face.

Ida and the doctor laughed. "Are you feelin' restless already, Jamie?" asked Ida.

Jamie nodded.

"I think it's best if you stay in bed today, and then I see no reason why you can't be up and about tomorrow," said Doc.

Ida asked, "What about his memory loss, Doc?"

Doc Fernald studied Jamie's face. Jamie tried not to look guilty, but as the doctor's kind blue eyes held his gaze, he felt a flush rise up his neck and head for his face.

At last the doctor spoke. "Well, there don't seem to be any signs of a concussion. So I think that when the boy is ready to remember, he will. Let's not worry too much about that right now."

CHAPTER 11

Jamie spent most of the day doing the crossword puzzle and re-reading the newspaper from back to front. After a hearty lunch of steaming chicken vegetable soup and a gooey grilled cheese sandwich on homemade sourdough bread, he felt like he was ninety-nine percent himself again.

Later that afternoon, Ida poked her head around the door. "Are you up for visitors, Jamie? There's some folks here who are mighty eager to see you."

"Absolutely!" Jamie plumped his pillows and sat up straighter in bed.

Christopher Pennysworth strode across the room, his hand extended and a white-toothed grin spread across his freckled face. His thick, pale gold hair stuck up in odd places as though he had just pulled off his cap.

"Good man!" Christopher said. He grasped Jamie's right hand between both of his own and shook it so vigorously that it resembled a dog excitedly wagging its tail. "Exceptional!"

Jamie couldn't help but grin back as Christopher yanked his hand up and down. "Thanks."

A tall, broad-shouldered man had followed Christopher into the room. He wore a gray wool coat that looked as soft as a blanket. Rich black velvet lined the collar and trimmed the pockets and cuffs, and shiny silver buttons formed a neat row down the front. A paisley scarf in shades of black, gray and cream draped over the man's shoulders. In his hand, he held a gray felt hat rimmed with a black silk band.

Dark circles shadowed soft gray eyes that almost matched the color of his coat. A neatly trimmed salt-and-pepper beard partially obscured a strong, square jaw. Suddenly a bright smile that mirrored Christopher's spread across the man's face. "I'm Robert Pennysworth," he said, extending his hand, "and you're the young man who saved our Kelly." Christopher released his grip on Jamie's hand, and Mr. Pennysworth replaced it with his own firm grasp. "I can never thank you enough."

"You're welcome, sir. I guess. I mean, it happened so fast that I didn't really have time to think about it."

Christopher said, "I'll say! I still don't know where you came from! I never even saw you dive into the water, and the next thing I knew you came shooting up holding onto my sister. It's as though you were already down there, like some kind of mermaid. Or merman rather."

Mr. Pennysworth said, "Well, wherever you came from, we are so very glad that you were there." His deep voice wavered and his words came out in a half whisper. Jamie could tell that he was choking back his emotions. "Honestly son, I don't even want to imagine what might have happened if you hadn't come along when you did. You are like an angel sent from heaven."

"How is Kelly?" Jamie asked. He felt a little embarrassed, especially since he hadn't purposely set out to be as heroic as he now appeared.

"This morning she sat up and had some broth. Right now she's weak, but she's a strong girl, and Doc says she'll regain strength quickly."

Jamie grinned. "Yes, she's strong all right, and tough for such a small girl. I saw her chasing after Christopher like Wayne Gretsky."

Christopher and Mr. Pennysworth exchanged puzzled looks. "Wayne who?" Christopher asked.

Jamie said, "Oh ... um ...he's a very famous hockey player where I come from."

Mr. Pennysworth asked, "Where is that?"

Jamie bit his lip. *Darn*, he thought, *I did it again*. He furrowed his brow and wrinkled his nose. "I ... I don't know. I mean, I can't remember much yet. I don't know why I remembered that name; it just sort of popped out."

"Well, then perhaps it's good sign," said Mr. Pennysworth. "Maybe it means your memory is starting to come back."

Ida said, "We've got Officer Leahy checkin' all around the county to find Jamie's folks, so I'll pass that name along and maybe it will help him out."

Good luck with that, thought Jamie.

Mr. Pennysworth turned to Ida. "Do you think that young Jamie will be well enough to come and see Kelly soon?"

"Can I, Ida?" Jamie leaned forward eagerly. "Do you think I could go tomorrow? I feel great now and another day in bed will just kill me!"

Ida laughed at the animated expression on Jamie's face. "Well, I'd say by your appetite and by the look of those roses in your cheeks that it just might be a possibility."

Christopher said, "Exceptional! You can play checkers with Kelly. She's easy to beat even when she isn't weak from almost drowning. And when I get home from school I can show you my room and the model I'm working on of Lindy's plane. It's ...."

"Exceptional?" Jamie asked.

Christopher beamed, his blue eyes twinkling. "Precisely!"

Mr. Pennysworth laid a hand on Christopher's shoulder. "Son, would you mind giving me a moment alone with Jamie?"

"Sure, Father. I'll wait downstairs. Maybe Ida will have a piece of pie she needs to dispose of, in which case, I'm just the man for the job!" He waved to Jamie as he headed out the door. "See you tomorrow, Jamie."

"Count on it," Jamie called back.

Mr. Pennysworth perched on the edge of the bed. His elegant fingers massaged the rim of his hat. He lifted his eyes and met Jamie's curious gaze. "Son," he began, but the words caught in his throat. He tried again. "Son, I can't even begin to tell you what it means to me – to us – what you did. We lost ... we lost ...." Mr. Pennysworth stopped. He took a deep breath and cleared his throat. "We lost Mrs. Pennysworth four years ago. I just don't know what would become of us if we had lost our Kelly too."

Mr. Pennysworth took a monogrammed handkerchief from his coat pocket and dabbed his eyes. "So you see, son, what you did for us was even more of a miracle than you may have thought." He stood up, buttoned his coat and said, "You get some rest now, Jamie. We want to see you up at our house as soon as possible. And thank you again, son. I mean that from the bottom of my heart."

Jamie didn't know what else to say, so he just said, "You're welcome."

After Mr. Pennysworth left, Jamie sat still for a long time. He thought about how sad it was that Mrs. Pennysworth had died. He couldn't imagine his own mother dying – it was the worst thought imaginable. Jamie fought back tears as he thought of his mom and grandparents and wondered what they were doing right now. Were they frantic with worry? He pictured his mother on the TV news, crying and pleading for him to come home. He had seen things like that before, but he had never understood how it really felt. Now Jamie was a missing person himself.

He slunk down under the covers. Exhaustion overwhelmed him, but even as his eyelids drooped, he formed a steely resolve. *I want to go home. I want to be with my mother and Grandma and Grandpa for Christmas. I have four days to figure out how to get back home, and I will find a way.*

CHAPTER 12

Muffled laughter woke Jamie at twilight. He rolled onto his stomach and looked out the window. The setting sun cast long, blue-gray shadows across the snowy yard. A sudden wind kicked loose snow into a swirl that zigzagged toward Vanderzee's. Jamie's gaze followed the swirl and lingered on the old building. With its boarded-up windows, the place looked like it had closed its eyes and gone to sleep.

His stomach growled and his left foot tingled with pins and needles. "I've been stuck in bed too long!" he declared to no one but himself. He couldn't help but wonder what people in 1932 did to entertain themselves when they were sick in bed for days at a time. Back home, he always had the television or his games and books to keep him busy.

Jamie jumped out of bed, hopping on his right foot and shaking the left foot awake. A blue bathrobe hung from a hook on the back of the bedroom door, so he put it on. He opened the top drawer of the bureau and found a pair of red wool socks. He put those on too.

He padded down the hallway and paused at the top of the stairs. The aroma of a baking ham floated up the stairwell. He heard the snap of the wood fire and saw its reflected flames dancing in the parlor windows. Voices drifted from the kitchen, rising and falling in a soft rhythm. He gripped the mahogany railing and stepped onto the top stair.

THUD! THUD! THUD! The front door shuddered with the force of someone pounding on it from outside. Jamie froze.

From the kitchen, Ida called, "I'll get it." A moment later, Jamie saw her fiery-red head bobbing through the parlor. She wiped her hands on her apron, gripped the brass doorknob and swung the door open. Her shoulders stiffened. "Hello, Jim, what can I do for you?" she asked, her tone uncharacteristically cold.

Intrigued, Jamie sat down on the stairs and pressed his face between the balusters.

The man named Jim said, "Me and my friend Pete need a place to stay."

The conversations in the kitchen ceased abruptly. For a moment, the house was so quiet that Jamie could hear the mantel clock ticking.

"I'm afraid I'm full up," Ida said.

Flickering firelight illuminated Jim's face. He had curly black hair, high, well-defined cheekbones and a strong, square jaw. Ebony eyes smoldered beneath thick, dark brows. He would have been handsome except for the cruel line of his mouth and the sneering expression on his face. Jim planted his palm on the front door and loomed over Ida, those black eyes glaring with the intensity of laser beams. Jamie felt a shiver run up his spine.

"You mean to say that you can't make room for just two more? We'll sleep on the floor, right over there by the fire."

"You're not welcome here, Jim Gordon. Not even to sleep on my floor," Ida said. Rusty came up behind her and placed his broad hand on her shoulder.

Jamie gasped. *Jim Gordon!* Jamie suddenly remembered that when Mom was telling him stories about Canterbury, she had said that Mr. Gordon left town to find work somewhere else. Now he was back.

Jim's eyes narrowed to slits. "Why not?" he hissed through clenched teeth.

"You know perfectly well why not. Do you think the people in this town are fools? We saw the bruises on Iris's arms. We know all about you, Jim Gordon."

Jim threw back his head and let out a howl of laughter. "Iris is as clumsy as a two-legged goat," he said. "Ain't my fault she's always bumpin' into things and bangin' herself up."

"No Jim. No one is that clumsy." Ida's tone was crisp and cold. "Now please go so we can have our supper."

Suddenly Jim's open palm became a fist. He slammed it into the door, knocking Ida's hand from the knob and sending her teetering backwards into Rusty. Jim spat out his next words. "Just who do you think you are anyway, the Queen of Canterbury?"

Rusty stepped between them. Fred, Roy, Harry, George, Big Ed and Little Ed gathered around too, creating a fortress of bodies for which Jim and Pete were no match. "You heard the lady, Jim," said Rusty. "You and your friend aren't welcome here. Time to move along now."

Jim shook his fist and shouted, "You'll be sorry! Both of you! All of you!"

As he turned to leave, Jim spotted Jamie perched at the top of the stairs. Nodding his head in the boy's direction, he asked, "What are you runnin' now, an orphanage?" All heads turned until everyone was looking up at Jamie. Jim's black eyes narrowed. "What do you think you're lookin' at, kid?" he growled.

Without thinking, Jamie answered, "Nothing much, mister."

"Out of the mouths of babes," said Ida, and she and the boarders moved together to force Jim back onto the porch. Rusty secured the door and slid the deadbolt into place.

"You haven't seen the last of me!" Jim yelled from outside.

The men gathered around Ida, who looked pale and shaken. Rusty squeezed her shoulders. "It's all right, Ida, we'll take turns keeping an eye out tonight."

Ida wiped her palms on her apron. "I'm not afraid of that young bully."

"No ma'am, we all know that. But it won't hurt to take a few precautions. Better safe than sorry."

Ida said, "You know, he never used to be like that."

George shook his head and said, "Hard times can change a man, for better or worse."

"If you ask me," said Rusty, "hard times don't change folks. Hard times just show what folks is already made of."

CHAPTER 12

Ida sighed. "Well, I think I'd better check on Iris tomorrow. It can't be good for her to have that piece of bad news back in town. She's been doin' just fine on her own since he left."

Rusty looked up at Jamie, whose face was still squeezed between the balusters. He motioned with his head toward the kitchen. "Well come on down here, son, and let's have our supper. Look's like the show's over for tonight."

CHAPTER 13

"King me!"

Kelly sank into her soft pink pillows and grinned.

Jamie placed one black checker on top of another. "I thought you weren't supposed to be good at this game," he said, frowning.

"Who told you that?" Kelly asked.

"Christopher."

Kelly smirked. "He was pulling your leg. Checkers is my game!"

"I guess it is! You've beaten me seven times in row."

"Eight, but who's counting?"

They had been playing all morning, ever since Jamie and Ida got to the Pennysworth house not long after breakfast. Ida had found Jamie a wool sweater, overcoat, boots, mittens and a scarf to wear for their trek up the hill. The sweater came almost to his knees and the coat almost to his ankles, but Ida said that he should be able to borrow something closer to his own size from Christopher. Jamie had noticed sled marks and toboggan trails crisscrossing the hill as they climbed. When they passed Vanderzee's, he had peeked at the place out of the corner of his eye. But in the bright morning sunshine it had only looked lonely and deserted, not particularly spooky.

As they neared the summit, the Pennysworth house had suddenly come into view. Jamie admired the wide front porch and fancy gingerbread trim, the colossal Christmas wreaths that adorned every window and door, and the garland that trimmed the elegant wrought-iron railings gracing each side of the wide brick steps.

The door had been answered by a young woman wearing a ruffled white apron over a blue plaid dress. She had large brown eyes, fair skin and rosy cheeks. From her dress and manner, Jamie assumed she was the Pennysworth's house-keeper. She smiled when she saw them and opened the door wide. "Ida! How wonderful to see you! Come in, come in."

Ida said, "Iris, this is Jamie. He's the young man who res-cued Kelly from the pond. Jamie, this is Mrs. Gordon."

Iris Gordon threw her arms around him. "Oh! *You're* the boy! It's an honor to meet you! I can't thank you enough for saving our girl. I don't know what would have become of poor Mr. Pennysworth if something had happened to that child."

Jamie blushed as Iris hugged him again before finally letting him go. He immediately ducked down to untie his boots. The hardwood floor smelled of lemon wax and was polished to such a glossy shine that he could see his reflec-tion in it. An elegant marble staircase, flanked by gleaming mahogany banisters, rose gracefully to the second floor. At the top, a balcony ran the full length of the second story landing. Gilt-framed portraits of people with stern faces and old-fashioned clothes lined the walls.

Ida whooshed past Iris and peered into what looked like a white wicker basket on wheels. "*OOOOH!* Is this our little Emilie? She's sleepin', precious thing. Look at those cunnin' pink cheeks. Jamie, come look!"

Soft white blankets covered the baby like a fluffy cloud. She had wispy, light brown curls, and a pink headband circled her head like a halo. One fist, no bigger than a silver dollar, was curled against her round chin. Jamie had never seen such tiny fingers.

Mrs. Gordon beamed. "Thank you. Mr. Pennysworth was kind enough to get this carriage so that I could keep Emilie with me at work. She's such a good baby, no trouble at all." Iris turned to Jamie. "I'm sure you don't want to stand around staring at a baby all day! Go on up to see Kelly. Her room is at the top of the stairs, third door down on the right."

"Okay, thanks." Jamie ran up the stairs. At the top he turned right, counted three doors and knocked.

"Come in!" Kelly sat in bed, her long blond hair woven into braids that fell over her shoulders. Her room was a symphony in pink – pink walls, pink polka dot curtains, pink plaid pillows, a furry pink rug and a pink flowered bedspread. There was a pink bureau, pink lamps and pink lamp shades. Kelly was wrapped up in pink and white striped blankets. Her pale oval face was like a white full moon floating in a very pink sky. Her blue eyes lit up when she saw him. "It's you!" she cried. "I'm so glad you've come!"

"How are you feeling?" Jamie asked.

"A little weak. And I get tired quickly. But I feel pretty good, considering. What about you?"

"Doc says I'm fine. So let me guess. Your favorite color is green, right?"

"Ha ha, very funny. Hey! You're a big hero, you know."

Jamie blushed. "Okay, I'm starting to find this hero stuff a little embarrassing."

"Well, then I guess we'll have to cancel the parade."

Jamie's eyes bugged. "Wh – what parade?"

Kelly giggled and said, "I'm teasing. Though we should have a parade in your honor, I think. Seriously though, thank you for saving me."

"You're welcome."

The morning had flown by as the two new friends played checkers and talked. Jamie marveled that he was having such a good time with someone he had just met – and a girl two years younger to boot. She reminded him of his friend Libby, who was the only girl on their soccer team, and the best goalkeeper in their league. Around noontime Kelly asked, "Would you mind going down and asking Mrs. Gordon if she would make us some lunch? I feel like grilled cheese and tomato soup."

Jamie hopped off the bed. "When I get to the bottom of the stairs, which way is the kitchen?"

"Turn left. You'll see a Butler's Pantry. Go through it and you'll be there."

Jamie was tempted to slide down the smooth, polished-to-a-sheen and very sturdy looking mahogany banister, but then he thought how embarrassed he would feel if Mrs. Gordon caught him. He turned left at the bottom of the stairs and walked through the pantry.

The kitchen was as big as the whole downstairs of Ida's Boarding House. A giant center island with a gleaming white marble top stretched the full length of the room. Above the island hung a huge wrought iron rack loaded with copper pans. Except for a yellow and white cat curled up on a stool, no one was there.

Voices drifted from beyond a partially-open door at the far end of the kitchen. Through a window in the door, Jamie saw Mrs. Gordon talking to someone who was just out of sight. "I need this job to support myself and Emilie," she cried, her voice sounding shaky and tense. "I'm lucky Mr. Pennysworth lets me bring the baby to work with me. I can't betray his trust."

"You'll do what I say, or you won't have a baby to worry about!"

Jamie gasped. He recognized that deep voice! It was that awful man from last night – Jim Gordon.

Iris pleaded, "You wouldn't hurt our baby. You wouldn't!" She started to sob.

Jamie tiptoed around the edge of the kitchen island. From here, he could see Jim's face hovering above Mrs. Gordon's like a dark storm cloud. "You have no idea what I would do!" Jim hissed, grabbing her wrist and twisting it. Iris' face contorted with pain and she cried out.

Jamie picked up the sleeping cat and gently placed it on the floor. "Sorry kitty," he whispered as the cat stretched, yawned and curled up again. Jamie climbed up on the stool and onto the counter. Holding his breath, he carefully lifted a frying pan from the overhead rack. He climbed back down and ducked behind the island.

"Jim! Stop it! You're hurting me!" Iris wailed.

With a knee-jerk reaction, Jamie banged the pan against the side of the cabinet.

"What was that?" Jim snarled.

Thinking fast, Jamie grabbed the cat and pushed it toward the back of the kitchen. The cat objected with an offended mew. "Sorry again, kitty," he whispered.

Someone came inside. Jamie squeezed his eyes shut and stayed completely still. For a moment the kitchen was as quiet as a church on Monday morning. Then the cat mewed again.

Iris said, "It's just the cat."

Thanks, kitty, Jamie thought as he crawled back into the pantry. He stood up, called out, "Mrs. Gordon?" and stepped into the kitchen.

"Hello Jamie." Iris's face looked flushed and her brown eyes were red-rimmed. She rubbed her right wrist with her left hand. "What do you need, dear?" Her voice sounded unsteady.

"Kelly wanted me to ask if you would make us lunch." Jamie smiled, trying to act like everything was normal. "She'd like tomato soup and grilled cheese, if you have it."

Iris opened a cabinet and pulled out a can of Campbell's tomato soup. "Her appetite is improving, that's a good sign," she said. "What have you two been up to all morning?"

"Playing checkers."

Iris' hand trembled as she cranked open the soup. She managed a wry smile and said, "Did she let you win any?"

Jamie rolled his eyes. "Not many."

Jim pushed the back door open and glared at them. "Hey, aren't you that smart-mouthed kid from the boardin' house?" His eyes were dark slits.

Iris spun around and spoke before Jamie could answer. "It was nice of you to come by, Jim, but I'm afraid you'll have to go now." Her voice sounded high-pitched, but steadier.

Jamie walked the length of the kitchen. "Here, let me close the door so the cold air doesn't come in. Goodbye, Mr. Gordon, it was nice to see you again," he said pleasantly, and began to shut the door in Jim's face.

A scarlet flush crept up Jim's neck. A vein in his left temple bulged and began to throb. His nostrils flared and his eyes looked dark and fierce. For a moment Jamie thought he might lunge through the door, but then Mr. Gordon jammed clenched fists into his pockets and turned away, muttering, "Kids! Nothin' but trouble, that's what they are."

As if on cue, Emilie began to wail. Jamie hadn't noticed her before, because she had been sleeping in her carriage in the far corner of the kitchen, next to a wooden rocking chair. Iris hurried over and picked her up. "There, there, sweet pea," she said, bouncing the baby gently and patting her back. Emilie belched and immediately stopped crying.

Jamie and Mrs. Gordon laughed. "I guess that's what she needed," Iris said. "Would you like to hold her?"

Jamie hesitated. "Okay …." he said, but it sounded more like a question than an answer. His Aunt Jess had let him hold his cousins Timmy and Petie when they were babies, but she always had him sit down first so he wouldn't drop them. "Can I sit in that rocking chair while I hold her?"

Iris smiled. "Take a seat." When Jamie was settled in the rocker Iris said, "Here, just put her in the crook of your arm with her head resting above your elbow, and use your other hand underneath to hold her, like this." She placed Emilie in Jamie's arms.

The baby felt soft and rubbery and smelled like applesauce. He smiled at her and she smiled back. One deep dimple creased her left cheek. She was so cute and helpless. *How could anyone threaten to hurt her?* he wondered.

"Hi there, Emilie, I'm Jamie." He looked at Iris. "I don't know what he's talking about, Mrs. Gordon. She's no trouble. No trouble at all."

CHAPTER 14

At three-thirty that afternoon, Christopher burst into Kelly's room, still wearing his coat and hat, his cheeks rosy and chapped. He skidded to a stop, pulled off his cap and bent over, hands to knees, panting. His words came out in spurts. "I. Ran. All the way. Home. I was. Hoping. You'd. Be here." Chris spotted the checkerboard on the bed and grinned. "How many. Times. Has. She. Beaten you?"

Jamie pretended to scowl. "I've lost count. You told me she wasn't any good at checkers."

"Ha! I was pulling your leg. She looks harmless enough, but she's a genius when it comes to games."

"Tell us about school!" Kelly cried.

Chris removed his coat and collapsed into a pink plaid chair. "Boy it smells good in here. What did you have for lunch?"

"Grilled cheese and Campbell's tomato soup," said Kelly. "Please tell us about school."

"Mm Mm Good!" said Christopher.

Kelly threw her hands up, exasperated. "Yes, it was Mm Mm Good! *NOW TELL US ABOUT SCHOOL!*"

"Okay, okay! No need to get your knickers in a twist!" Chris said. "We had the spelling bee today."

"Who won?" Kelly asked.

"It was a real cliffhanger, but in the end, Frannie MacDonald beat out Teddy Preble."

"That's two in a row for Frannie! What was the winning word?"

"Onomatopoeia, which for your information is spelled o-n-o-m-a-t-o-p-O-e-i-a! Who would ever have thought to put that fourth O in there? Anyway, it came right down to the wire because Teddy was looking like a favorite to win after he managed to spell Leishmaniasis."

"What the heck is that?" Jamie asked.

"Good question! Teddy asked them to use it in a sentence, and turns out it's some sort of dreadful disease caused by parasites. It's named for this fellow, Sir William Boog Leishman, who discovered it."

"Boog?" Kelly and Jamie asked at the same time, and burst out laughing.

Still giggling, Kelly asked, "Is he the person they named the *Boog*-ey man for?"

"No ... no ... I think he's the man they named *Boog*-ers for," said Jamie, and they laughed so hard that both Jamie and Chris dropped to the floor and rolled around holding their sides. Every time they tried to stop, they burst out laughing again. Kelly laughed so hard she got hiccups, which just made them laugh all the more. Jamie suddenly realized that it had been quite a long time since he'd had a good laugh with friends, or even just a good laugh, period.

When at last they exhausted themselves, Chris said, "But that wasn't even the most exciting part of the day."

"What, there's more?" Jamie asked, still holding his sides. "I don't think I can take any more!"

Kelly leaned forward and said, "Tell us."

Christopher climbed back into the chair. Jamie rolled onto his belly and rested his chin in his hands. "Okay, I'm ready too. Tell us."

"At lunch recess, Wally Winchester and Goosey Thompson got into a tussle, something to do with whether or not the Three Wise Men were all that wise. Goosey said that *real* wise men wouldn't just set off following a star, and Walter said that it proved they were wise because they had faith that there would be something good waiting for them at the end of the journey. They went back and forth about it and the next thing you know Wally said something about Goosey's father being a Socialist and Goosey said that was better than being a Capitalist —look what they've done for the country! Wally shoved Goosey and they ended up rolling around on the ground, pulling each other's hair and throwing punches that never seemed to land anywhere, until Mrs. Lindstrom and Mr. Malone pulled them apart. It was all quite spectacular!"

Just as Chris finished his story, there was a rap on the door. Iris Gordon poked her head into the room. "Sounds like about as much fun as the circus in here," she said, eyeing their flushed faces and happy expressions. "You three seem like you've known each other for ages."

Kelly said, "That's how it feels to me too."

Iris said, "I came up to tell you that your father is going to be late this evening. He has to meet with a bank client over in Bell's Crossing. Mrs. Watson will come by later to make your supper. I'll stay until she gets here."

Jamie gasped. His eyes grew as round as chestnuts and his heart pounded like a tom-tom. For a moment, he felt like time had stopped.

"Good grief, Jamie. What's wrong?" Chris asked. "You look like you've been struck by lighting."

Jamie's mind whirled, but he couldn't speak because his lips and tongue felt paralyzed. *Bell's Crossing, she had said! Mr. Pennysworth was going to Bell's Crossing!* At last he managed to gulp out a few words. "Is that Bell's Crossing, *Vermont?*"

Iris, Kelly and Chris exchanged glances. Iris said, "Yes, that's right."

"What's wrong, Jamie?" Kelly asked.

"I – I've heard of Bell's Crossing."

"You *have?* You mean that you remember something? Something about Bell's Crossing?"

"I – I guess so. I'm just a little confused. Is it near here?"

"It's about fifteen miles south of Canterbury," Chris said. "We went through there on our way to Boston when we went to a Red Sox game at Fenway Park last summer."

Jamie's mind raced. "So, then … you mean … Canterbury is a *real place?*"

Kelly furrowed her brow and said, "Of course it's a real place, silly! We're *here* aren't we?"

CHAPTER 15

Of course it's a real place! Of course it's a real place! The words echoed inside Jamie's head.

"Maybe Doc Fernald should take another look at that bump on your head," Christopher said, eyeing Jamie's glazed expression with concern. He poked Jamie's shoulder with his index finger. "Jamie?"

Of course it's a real place! Suddenly Jamie jumped up. "I've got to go!" he cried.

He headed for the door, but Chris grabbed his arm and pulled him back. "Hang on a second; I'm supposed to give you some better-fitting clothes to wear." Chris sprinted from the room before Jamie could object.

Jamie shifted from one foot to the other and back again. He tried to look calm, but his stomach bounced up and down as though he had swallowed Mexican jumping beans. *Of course it's a real place!* The words replayed over and over in his mind like an annoying song. Just when he thought Chris would never return, a large pile of clothes with legs appeared at the bedroom door. Chris dropped the clothes on the floor and said, "Here's a Woolrich jacket that should do nicely and a pair of practically-new boots from L.L. Bean. And some other things too."

Jamie pulled on the boots and shoved his arms into the jacket sleeves. He didn't care if anything fit; he just wanted to get out of there. He loaded up with a navy blue wool sweater, two flannel shirts and a pair of gray wide-wale corduroys. "Thanks, Christopher, this is great. I'll see you guys tomorrow!" he shouted as he ran out the door. Kelly called after him, but Jamie kept moving. He flew down the marble stairs and barreled through the front door.

Outside at last, Jamie gulped in the fresh, cold air. He sat down on the front steps, his mind churning like an overloaded washing machine. *Of course it's a real place!* Grandma had never once mentioned that her Christmas Village was modeled after a real place. All along, Jamie believed that he had been transported into an imaginary world that had magically become real. But now he wondered, *what if what's really happened is that I've traveled back in time to the* real *Canterbury that existed in 1932, with all the* real *people that actually lived there – here – then?*

Jamie stood up and trudged down the hill, clutching his heap of borrowed clothing to his chest. He sighed. *Now I'm more confused than ever about how to get back home.* His mind circled around the problem, trying to sort it out and alternating between confusion and despair. He felt utterly helpless and alone. Sure, most of the people in Canterbury were kind and caring. Ida, Rusty and the men at the boarding house were great. Doc Fernald, Mr. Pennysworth and Mrs. Gordon were nice too. And he felt like he had known Kelly and Christopher forever. But if he told his new friends the truth, would they believe him? Jamie huddled inside his borrowed Woolrich jacket. *No, they wouldn't. And neither would I, if I were in their shoes.*

Boys and girls on sleds, flying saucers and toboggans whizzed past him, screaming and hollering all the way down the hill. The smell of a bonfire filled the air. Children gathered around it, talking, laughing and toasting marshmallows on long sticks. Jamie watched them pop the blackened masses of goo into their mouths and lick their sticky fingers. He remembered times when he had felt that happy and carefree, and he envied them.

As he passed Vanderzee's, a banging noise jolted him from his funk. Jamie stared at the foreboding structure that seemed to demand his attention every chance it got. It towered like an impenetrable stone fortress, with dead vines creeping over its ramparts like woody tentacles. For a moment everything was still. Then the wind howled, and a loose board flapped against the side of the building. *I guess that's all it was.*

Just then, light flickered in a first story window. Jamie froze, every nerve in his body on full alert. The sun dipped lower in the sky and he realized that it had only been the reflection of the setting sun in a sliver of window glass peeking between the boards. A cold wind brushed across his cheek like a witch's kiss, sending shivers up and down his spine. He burrowed his face in his armload of clothes and sprinted the rest of the way to Ida's.

CHAPTER 16

That evening, Jamie peeled potatoes while Ida picked meat off of a roasted chicken that smelled so good it made his stomach growl. He moved slowly and mechanically, like a robot in a hypnotic daze.

"Penny for your thoughts," said Ida, as she separated white meat and dark meat into separate bowls.

Her words startled him. He remembered his mother saying those very words just, what was it, two, three days ago? All of a sudden, time had taken on a strange, unpredictable quality. It no longer flowed along in a nice straight line from past to present. Instead, it jumped around willy-nilly, from 2007 to 1932, from the day after tomorrow to the day before yesterday. Jamie remembered his sullen response in the car on the way to Grandma and Grandpa's house, and felt ashamed.

"I was thinking about time," he finally answered.

"Time? What about time?" Ida cocked her head and peeked at him out of the corner of her eye.

Jamie scraped the vegetable peeler across the last potato. "Well, a lot of things really. I was thinking that I've only been here for two days, but it seems like much longer. I feel like I've known you all forever." He pushed the bowl of potatoes to the side and started peeling carrots. "And then I was thinking about how, *before*, I was always wishing for time to jump ahead for something, like summer vacation. But then some bad stuff happened and I started wishing I could turn time back to before everything changed. Now I just keep wishing for time to slow down so that I can figure out how to get home in time for Christmas."

Ida stopped what she was doing and turned to face him. "That's quite a lot of thinkin' you've been doin'. Sounds like maybe you've started rememberin' things?"

Jamie hesitated. He wanted to tell her everything, but he was afraid. At the same time, he felt bone-weary from hiding the truth. Still intently peeling a carrot, he said, "Yes ma'am, I have."

Just then the front door banged open. "Give us a hand here, fellas," called Fred.

"Got us a Christmas tree," Rusty announced. "She's a beauty!"

Jamie and Ida watched as Big Ed and Little Ed ran to help Rusty and Fred haul in an eight foot evergreen with snowy branches. At first Jamie had constantly confused the two Eds, until Harry explained that Big Ed was so-called because he wasn't, and Little Ed was so-called because he was. Jamie still wasn't sure any of it made sense, but it had somehow helped him know which Ed was which.

"Where'd you get it?" asked Roy.

Rusty stood the tree upright in the middle of the parlor. "Over to Bascomb's woods. He's letting folks cut their own trees for free this year, seeing as times is so hard."

"That's real nice of him," said Ida. "Let's let it dry out over in that corner so it's not too near the fire. I'll get the decorations out of the attic in the mornin', and tomorrow night we can decorate it."

Back in the kitchen, Jamie finished peeling the carrots. "What else can I do?" he asked.

Ida handed him an onion. "Sorry for the bad news, dear, but I need you to peel this for me."

Jamie wrinkled his nose and held the onion at arm's length. Gingerly he picked off the first layer of papery skin. He winced as the onion's pungent odor instantly brought tears to his eyes.

Rusty wandered into the kitchen and peeked over Ida's shoulder. Before she could stop him, he swiped a piece of dark chicken meat and popped it into his mouth. "Oh boy, that's good, Ida. Moist, tender, seasoned to perfection, as always."

Ida slapped his hand. "Ooh, *You!*" she cried, puffing out her cheeks. "Keep your hands out of that bowl or there won't be enough for supper."

Rusty winked at Jamie behind Ida's back. "Yes Ma'am," he said with mock remorse. "Oh, by the way! I ran into Officer Leahy today. He said he's been checking around about Jamie in nearby towns, but nothing's turned up yet. Don't worry though, he's a good man and he'll keep at it."

Ida tilted her head and gave Jamie a sidelong glance. "Jamie, want to tell Rusty what we were just talkin' about?" she asked.

Jamie took a deep breath and blew it out with a whoosh. He wasn't sure what would come out of his mouth next, but he knew that he couldn't keep things inside much longer. At last he said, "We were talking about time. And about how I'm starting to remember things."

"Like what? Anything we should pass on to Officer Leahy?"

Jamie shook his head. "No, nothing like that. It's just that I remember that my dad did something bad. He invested people's money for them, but he made bad investments and lost a lot of it. He tried to hide what happened, hoping he could make it all back before anyone found out. But he just kept losing money and finally he couldn't hide it anymore."

Ida said, "I guess there's been a lot of that kind of thing goin' on in recent times."

Jamie wanted to say, yes, *but this didn't happen in recent times, it happened seventy-five years from now*. He wiped tears from his eyes. "I'm not crying because of what I just told you. It's the onion."

"So what happened?" Rusty asked.

"He ran off and left us. He wrote us a note saying that he hadn't meant to do anything wrong, but it all got out of control. He said he was sorry for everything and that he thought it would be better for us if he just disappeared." Jamie's tears flowed freely now. "But I think he was just afraid of going to jail."

CHAPTER 16

Ida pulled a handkerchief from her apron pocket and handed it to him.

"So he ran away from his troubles," Rusty said.

"Uh huh." Jamie wiped his eyes and gave the handkerchief back to Ida.

"Did you run away too?" Rusty's voice was gentle.

"No! I mean, I don't think so … well, at least not on purpose. What I really wanted was for everything to go back to the way it had been before. I wanted to turn back time. Then I started wishing that I could go someplace where nobody knew about the stuff with my dad. But I didn't *mean* to run away. It just happened. One minute I was home, and the next, I was in the pond. I know that sounds unbelievable, but it's true."

There, he'd said it. At least most of it. Jamie didn't have any more answers than he had before, but inside he felt lighter.

"We believe you, son," Rusty said, gently placing his large, callused palm on Jamie's shoulder and giving it a squeeze.

"Anyway, now I think that maybe Dad was really scared and thought nobody would understand." Jamie picked the last bit of skin from the onion, leaving it pearly and white. "But I've been thinking about it a lot, and it seems to me that it would have been a whole lot better if he had just asked somebody for help."

"I guess that's a lesson for all of us," said Ida.

"Amen to that," said Rusty.

CHAPTER 17

It was barely nine o'clock when Jamie knocked on the Pennysworth's front door the next morning. He bounced up and down, mentally chanting, *c'mon, c'mon, c'mon,* as he willed Mrs. Gordon to hurry.

At last she swung the door open. "Good morning!" Iris said. "We've been worried about you! You seemed upset when you left us yesterday."

"I know. I'm sorry about that. I got up here as fast as I could to let you know that I'm fine now." Jamie stepped into the foyer. "Really."

"I'm glad you're all right," Iris said, closing the door behind him. "I know Kelly is anxious to see you."

"Is Christopher here too?"

"No, he went to the bank with his father this morning. Mr. Pennysworth is teaching him about financial things. Chris said to tell you that he'll be home for lunch, and this afternoon he'll show you around the village."

"Sounds good." Jamie hopped on his right foot and tugged off his left boot. He switched feet, and as soon as both boots were off, made a beeline for the stairs. "I'll see you later, Mrs. Gordon," he said, scaling the marble steps two at a time.

"Oh, Jamie!" Iris called, just as he rounded the turn at the top of the stairs. Jamie skidded to a stop and peered over the balcony. "Nurse Carpenter is coming by to see Kelly this morning. Please tell her that she'll be here around ten o'clock."

"Will do," he said and ran down the hallway.

"I thought you'd never get here!" Kelly cried when he burst through her doorway. "I was worried you wouldn't come. You left in such a hurry yesterday! Are you all right?"

"I'm fine," Jamie said. "I'm sorry I ran off like that. Like I told Mrs. Gordon, I couldn't wait to get up here this morning to let you know that I'm okay. I've been awake since four and ready to go since six, but Ida said it isn't polite to knock on people's doors before nine. So I helped her make pancakes, then I helped her clean up the dishes, then I swept the ashes from the fireplace and got some up my nose, then I took the garbage out to the compost heap behind the barn, made my bed and brought in more firewood."

"That's a whole day's work!" Kelly said, laughing.

Jamie sprawled across the foot of her bed and rested the back of one hand against his forehead. "Tell me about it! I'm exhausted, so go easy on me with the checkers."

"Oh, don't be so dramatic," Kelly said as she lifted the checkerboard from her bedside table and placed it on her lap. "Remember, *I'm* the one who almost drowned."

"And just how long do you think you'll be able to milk that one?" he asked, grinning.

She narrowed her almond-shaped blue eyes and smirked. "As long as I can get away with it."

"Oh! I forgot to tell you! Mrs. Gordon said the nurse will be here soon."

"Then we better get busy." Kelly slapped her red checkers onto the board and rubbed her palms together like a villain in a silent movie. By the time Nurse Carpenter arrived, Kelly was ahead three games to one.

"Saved by the nurse," Jamie said.

Kelly said, "There's a game room at the other end of the house. We have a pool table if you want to play. Come back in – how long, Nurse Carpenter – half an hour?"

"That should be about right," Nurse Carpenter said.

Jamie strolled down the wide, grand hallway, pausing to study the portraits lining the wall. He saw a resemblance in many of them to Christopher and Kelly, with their thick golden hair and the startling blue eyes. But the ancestors looked rather grim compared to his friends. *I wonder why they never smiled back then. Maybe they all had really bad teeth. Or wooden teeth.*

He stopped in front of a huge picture window that offered a view of the town. Mid-morning sun glinted off the pond, which looked barren and forlorn without skaters. A fire engine with its ladder fully extended was parked on the corner by the common. A man clung precariously to the end of the ladder, attempting to toss strings of Christmas lights onto the upper branches of the giant pine tree. On the ground below, a man with his hands cupped around his mouth seemed to be shouting instructions to the man above. He suddenly waved his arms back and forth in front of his face as if to say, "No, no, no, you've got it all wrong!" The man on the ladder threw his hands up as if to ask, "Now what am I doing wrong?" The lights he had been holding tumbled to earth. The man on the ground dropped to his knees, held his head in his hands, and shook it from side to side as if to say, "Why must I deal with fools?" Watching them, Jamie grinned.

His gaze traveled down Main Street, where a man was moving a stepladder from street lamp to street lamp, hanging big red bows from each one. Jamie experienced a sudden flash of déjà vu, as it dawned on him that he was watching Canterbury evolve bit by bit, detail by detail, into the scene in Grandma's Christmas Village. From what he could remember, the only things missing now were the carolers beneath the tree and a black Scottish terrier with a red plaid bow sniffing at a snowman near the pond. Jamie's stomach squirmed, and he had the uneasy feeling that his time to figure out how to get back home was running out.

CHAPTER 18

Lost in thought, Jamie continued down the hallway in search of the game room. Movement caught his eye as he passed an open door. He stopped, poked his head around the doorjamb and found himself looking into a large bedroom with a high ceiling and a thick white carpet. A four-poster bed with a white fringed bedspread and matching canopy sat between floor-to-ceiling windows flanked by blue velvet drapes.

On the wall to his right hung a portrait of a beautiful blond, blue-eyed woman wearing a sapphire-blue evening gown. Jamie immediately saw the resemblance to Kelly and realized that it must be a portrait of the late Mrs. Pennysworth.

The faint scent of perfume floated to him. Iris Gordon stood near a dressing table that had a white ruffled skirt and an oval mirror. On the table sat an assortment of old-fashioned perfume bottles with atomizers and a large silver box. Mrs. Gordon held a perfume bottle in front of her face and seemed to be sniffing the air.

Just as Jamie was about to call hello, Iris put down the bottle and opened the silver box. She lifted out a strand of pearls and dangled it from her fingers. After a moment, she put it back. She pulled out something smaller and held it up to the light. Jamie saw that it looked like a brooch with dazzling green and red stones that sparkled and sent rainbows dancing across the wall. Mrs. Gordon stood motionless for what seemed like a long time. Then, still holding the brooch, she slipped her hand into her apron pocket. When she pulled her hand out again, the brooch was gone.

CHAPTER 19

Jamie's heart hammered so hard that he was sure Mrs. Gordon could hear it all the way across the room. He froze, figuring out what to do next. Just then, she walked over to the bed, sat down, covered her face with her hands and began to cry.

"Mrs. Gordon?" Jamie said softly.

Iris' head jerked up and she looked at him like a startled deer caught in the headlights of a car. She quickly wiped the tears from her face. "How long have you been standing there?" she asked, her voice shaking.

"Only a second. Are you all right?"

She bit her lower lip and nodded yes, but her face crumpled. Her whole body trembled, until the sobs gushed out like an erupting volcano and tears spilled down her cheeks like Niagara Falls.

Jamie crossed the room and sat down beside her. "I guess I'll have to take that as a no," he said.

Mrs. Gordon's sobs came so fast now that she had to gasp for breath in between. Jamie felt awkward and uncomfortable, but he wanted to help. "Is it because of Mr. Gordon? I over-heard what he said to you yesterday."

Iris lifted her face and looked at him with surprise in her red-rimmed brown eyes. It reminded him of the way his mother had looked the morning they left for Bell's Crossing, so sad and yet trying to be brave. He felt a lump rise in his throat. "That was me that made the banging noise in the kitchen," he confessed.

"I wondered," she said, her voice choking between sobs.

"I heard Mr. Gordon say that he would hurt Emilie if you didn't help him. Does he want money?"

She nodded.

"Do you mind if I ask you something?"

Iris shook her head. She pulled a handkerchief from her right apron pocket and blew her nose. She took some deep breaths that seemed to help calm her.

"Well, you seem like a very nice person. So...." Jamie's voice trailed off as he struggled to find words that wouldn't insult her.

"So why did I marry a man like Jim?"

"Yeah."

Iris took another deep breath and composed herself. "Believe it or not, he wasn't always like that. He was hand-some and charming and fun."

Jamie's eyebrows shot up. He found it hard to picture the angry man who had threatened Ida and twisted Iris's wrist as someone who had once been thought of as charming and fun.

Iris continued. "When the market crashed in '29, Jim's father lost everything. He had to sell their house and his hardware store to pay off their debts. It crushed him, and in the fall of 1930 he died of a sudden stroke. Jim's mother took it hard and died three months later. After that Jim changed. He turned angry and bitter. And mean. I thought that when he found out we were going to have Emilie, things would get better, but I was wrong. I told him he had to go, and until yesterday, I hadn't seen him for eight months." Iris dabbed her eyes again. "I'm sorry. I shouldn't be telling you all this. You're just a child."

Jamie was quiet for a moment. Then he said, "Can I tell you something, Mrs. Gordon?"

"Of course."

"I know I'm only twelve, but believe it or not, I kind of do understand." He swallowed, summoning the courage to go on. "My dad used to be a good guy too, but he got himself in trouble and he changed."

Iris raised her eyebrows. "I thought you couldn't remember anything."

Jamie screwed up his face. "I know. I kind of lied about that. I mean, I do remember some stuff, but not everything." Jamie told her about the bad investments his father made with other people's money and how he had run off when everyone found out.

When he finished, Iris said, "I'm so sorry Jamie. Is that why you ran away?"

He cocked his head and looked at her. "Rusty thought I ran away too."

"Didn't you?"

"I didn't mean to. I just wanted so badly for things to be like they were before. I was happier at my grandparents' house, because I thought we had escaped from all the bad stuff. Turns out we hadn't. The next thing I knew, I woke up in Canterbury and I'm still not sure how I got here."

Mrs. Gordon placed her hand over his. "I'm sorry, Jamie. You shouldn't have to deal with things like that at your age."

Jamie squeezed back tears. "Mrs. Gordon?"

"Yes Jamie?"

"Do you think that maybe ... someday ... Mr. Gordon might change back to the way he used to be? You know, be a good person again?"

Iris shook her head. "I don't know, Jamie. I just know that I just can't trust him anymore."

"Oh." Jamie hunched his shoulders, crossed his arms over his chest and hugged his elbows.

Iris added quickly, "But Jamie, that doesn't mean that it's the same for your dad. He made mistakes, but there's still a chance he'll change his mind and make things right."

Jamie wanted to believe her, but he didn't feel convinced. A tear landed on his knee and he covered the spot with his hand. He stared down at his stocking feet and shuffled them against the rug. "There's something else that's been bothering me," he said.

"What's that?"

"I've been kind of worried that maybe I'm not such a nice person either. I mean, I've been so angry at my dad, and all I thought about was how he ruined *my* life and how bad *I* felt." He shook his head, remembering. "I took it out on my mother. I was really mean to her. I hardly talked to her at all, and when I did, I said awful things that I wish I could take back now."

Iris spoke gently. "Jamie, just because your dad didn't do the right things doesn't mean you're going to be just like him. In fact, we already have proof that people can count on you to do *exactly* the right thing when times get tough."

"What do you mean?"

"Jamie, you risked your life to save a little girl you'd never even met! I think that automatically makes you a good person."

"I never thought about it that way." Jamie felt his spirits lift. "Thanks, Mrs. Gordon, that really helps a lot." He stood up, ready to go, then paused and said, "I'm sure that Ida and Mr. Pennysworth would help if you asked them."

Iris smiled and said, "Are you sure you're only twelve? You seem terribly grown-up."

"I wish my mom could hear you say that! Well, I guess I'll go see if Nurse Carpenter is finished with Kelly."

"You run along. I just need to finish straightening up in here."

"Mrs. Gordon?"

"Yes, Jamie?"

"I hope you're right about me."

"I'm sure that I am, Jamie. In fact, I've never been more certain about anything."

CHAPTER 20

After checking to make sure he was alone in the hallway, Jamie turned the knob on the first door he found. It was a utility closet filled with brooms and dust pans and cleaning rags. He slipped inside and closed the door behind him, squeezing between a dust mop and a push broom and almost knocking over a pail. In the cramped space, the overpowering smells of furniture polish and disinfectant made him gag. He held his nose, breathed through his mouth and waited.

A moment later, he heard Mrs. Gordon's heels clack down the marble stairs. He waited another minute, then cracked open the closet door. When he was sure the coast was clear, he tiptoed back to the bedroom where he and Mrs. Gordon had talked. He paused in the doorway, torn between his overwhelming curiosity and his worry about being seen. He checked the hallway again. No one. Sunshine poured through the tall bedroom windows. A trace of perfume lingered in the air. Jamie scampered to the dressing table and looked down at the silver box. He glanced around one more time to make sure he was alone. Then he lifted the lid. His breath escaped with a soft whistle and he rolled his eyes upward. Iris had returned the brooch to the box, where it rested in a bed of blue silk, its emeralds and rubies sparkling in the late morning sun.

CHAPTER 21

"Do you want to go tobogganing, or would you like a tour of the spectacular sights of our fair village?" asked Christopher. He had returned from helping his father at the bank just in time to join Kelly and Jamie for another round of grilled cheese and tomato soup served on trays in Kelly's room.

"How about if we ride the toboggan to the bottom and then you can show me around?" Jamie offered.

Kelly sighed and said, "I can't believe tomorrow is Christmas Eve! I hope Father will let me go out. I'm feeling much better and it would just kill me to miss a Canterbury Christmas Eve!"

"What's so special about a Canterbury Christmas Eve?" Jamie asked.

Christopher explained, "At nine o'clock, the whole town gathers on the common. There's hot cider and Christmas goodies made by the women from the church Altar Guild. We light a huge bonfire and sing carols. At eleven they light up the tree and everyone says, *"OOOH"* and *"AAAAHHH,"* and then we hand out gifts to all the children. Just before midnight, we sing "Silent Night". The bells chime twelve, everyone says, 'Merry Christmas!' and we all go home, like Cinderella. The End!" Christopher threw his arms wide and bowed with a flourish.

Jamie laughed, but his stomach started bouncing up and down again. He was getting more worried by the minute. The magic that brought him to Canterbury had happened just as it was turning Christmas Eve in 2007. Jamie didn't understand how this whole time travel thing worked, but in his gut he felt certain that he had to get back home before Christmas Eve, 1932, was over.

Jamie promised Kelly that he would be there early the next morning, grabbed his jacket, and followed Christopher down a back stairway to the mudroom. They bundled up with scarves, mittens and hats and stepped outside into brilliant sunshine. Momentarily blinded, Jamie squinted to watch the colorful moving dots that were actually people on sleds zigzagging all over the hill. He inhaled deeply. The air smelled like Christmas in Vermont, clean and piney.

Christopher's toboggan leaned against the side of the house. "Father gave it to me for Christmas last year. It's faster than Lindy's plane!" Jamie tucked in tightly behind Chris and gripped the side ropes. Cold air slapped his face as they flew down the hill, leaning left and then right, swerving to dodge bushes and other people sledding. They hit a mound and flew high in the air before landing with a thump that bruised their backsides. They screamed "OW!" and howled with laughter at the same time.

Christopher tied the toboggan to a chestnut tree and the boys walked into town. He pointed out the Canterbury Savings Bank where Mr. Pennysworth worked and the hardware store that used to belong to the Gordon Family. They ducked into the Canterbury General Store, which reminded Jamie of the one in Bell's Crossing. It had the same musty smell and rough-hewn floorboards that creaked underfoot. Christopher bought them each a peppermint candy cane, plus one to take home for Kelly.

The sun cast afternoon shadows across the sidewalk as they continued their tour of the village. Jamie noticed that, even though tomorrow was Christmas Eve, Canterbury wasn't bustling with activity the way Bell's Crossing had been. He realized that it must be because it was the Depression and people didn't have much money to spend.

In the town square, Christopher pointed out the Civil War monument. "There's a great story about our statue. Do you notice anything strange about it?"

Jamie sucked on his candy cane, savoring its sticky peppermint flavor. He studied the fifteen-foot-tall gray stone statue of a soldier carrying a musket, shrugged and said, "Nope, I don't see anything odd about it."

"Look at his uniform!"

Jamie looked more closely and shrugged again. "Nope. I still don't see anything."

"He's a *Confederate* soldier! The town commissioned a statue of a Union soldier, of course, but they delivered this fellow instead. No one even noticed until after it was up and they had planted flowers all around it. After they realized the mistake, people were very upset, especially because Vermont was the first state to abolish slavery. But then someone suggested that we change the dedication, and that made most everyone feel better about it. Somewhere down in Virginia, there's a town with our Union soldier standing in the square."

Jamie read aloud the words chiseled into the statue's granite base. "This monument is dedicated to all who died in battle and to the thousands of our brothers and sisters freed from slavery in the War Between the States. May we never again place another living soul in human bondage and may we live hereafter united in brotherhood and peace." He paused, taking in the words. "You're right, Chris. That *is* a good story."

The boys approached the intersection of Main Street and Town Road. Across the street was the pond, and beside them the village common. The men he'd seen hanging the Christmas tree lights yesterday were now turning them on and off repeatedly, checking to make sure that all the lights worked, and bickering the whole time. Jamie grinned and said, "They're still at it."

"That's Jake and Rodney. They're the handymen for the town." Chris tipped his head toward Jamie and whispered, "They're *always* like that."

Jamie noticed a signpost with arrows pointing north, south, east and west. The south-pointing arrow read, "BELL'S CROSSING 15 MILES." A surge of homesickness hit him like a tidal wave.

Chris and Jamie crossed the street and walked toward the pond. Signs reading, "DANGER! THIN ICE!" warned them not to get too close to the edge. Nearby, two young boys had rolled one giant snowball and were starting on a second.

"Looks like the hole in the ice is mending," Christopher said. "But I don't think they'll let us go out on it any time soon." He picked up a stone and threw it side-arm, making it skip and hop over the ice. Jamie gazed across the pond to the snowy fields beyond and thought, *somewhere out there is home.*

"Okay! Just one more for the head and we're done," called one of the young boys. Jamie turned to watch as they rolled a third snowball, patted it with their mittens and carried it over to their snowman. The taller boy stretched on tiptoes to put the head in place, but he was just a hair too short.

"Here, let me help you with that," Jamie said. He placed the snowman's head carefully on top and packed snow around the neck to secure it.

Just then, the church bells chimed once for the half hour. "Jiminy Cricket! It's four thirty already!" said the smaller boy. "It'll be getting dark soon. We'll have to finish him up tomorrow. I can bring a carrot for his nose and coal for his eyes and mouth."

The taller boy said, "Bring enough for buttons down the front too. I'll bring my dad's old Princeton scarf and a hat."

Jamie's stomach lurched as he realized that he had just helped build the snowman in Grandma's Christmas Village scene. His blood felt cold and he imagined that he could actually feel it flowing through his veins like sand through an hour glass. He glanced back at the snowman and knew with certainty that when he saw it again, it would be wearing a bright orange scarf with a large black "P" on one end, and a black top hat on its head.

CHAPTER 22

"I guess we better get going too." Chris said. The boys retraced their steps down Main Street, walking a little faster this time, their shoulders hunched against the cold that deepened along with the late-day shadows. They spotted the handymen, Jake and Rodney, heading down the street, laughing and slapping each other's backs like the best of pals.

As the boys passed the Canterbury General Store, a man with a scraggly beard and a gaunt, weather-beaten face approached. He wore socks as gloves and appeared to have newspapers stuffed inside his torn and dirty jacket. Jamie hung back as the man drew near.

"Thpare a dime for thum thoop?" asked the raggedy-looking man.

Chris dug in his pocket and came up with a dime. "Here you go." Chris pulled out the candy cane that he'd gotten for Kelly. "Here, take this too. And this ...." He took off his scarf and gave it to the man, who grinned, revealing the cause of his lisp – a large space where his top front teeth should have been.

"Thankth, thon." The man wrapped the scarf around his neck and tucked the ends inside his coat. He adjusted the drape slightly and turned this way and that, admiring his reflection in the store window. "Bleth you, boyth. And Merry Chrithmuth," he said, and went on his way.

"That was nice of you," Jamie said. "I was a little afraid of him at first."

Chris said, "For all we know, a few years ago he could have been a successful businessman. Or a decorated war veteran. These days, there's no way to tell. Everyone hasn't been as lucky as we have. I just hope he doesn't use that dime to get swacked."

"Swacked?"

"Snookered. Tanked."

Jamie looked at Chris like he was speaking Chinese. "You've never heard those words?" Chis asked. "Where are you from, the dark ages?"

Jamie shrugged. "Something like that."

"It means drunk," Chris explained.

Jamie thought for a moment, remembering something he had learned in Mrs. Barrett's history class. "Isn't this, whaddyacallit, Prohibition?"

"Yup," Chris answered.

"So, how would he get it?"

Chris shrugged. "If he wanted to, he could buy moonshine somewhere."

Jamie glanced over his shoulder. He saw the hobo walk to the corner, where he disappeared into a doorway beneath a sign that read, *Aunt Polly's Kitchen*.

Jamie smiled and said, "Nope, he's not getting smacked."

"Swacked."

"Right, swacked."

The boys reached the base of the hill where Christopher had tied up his toboggan. Less than a hundred yards away, Vanderzee's cast its somber gray shadow over the snow. Jamie said, "I've been having dreams about that place. I was inside."

"How did you know it was Vanderzee's?"

"Because I saw the sign when I escaped and got outside."

Christopher cocked his head and eyed the building. "Believe it or not, I've never been in there. What was it like in your dreams?"

"Dark. And cold." Jamie shivered, remembering. "Someone was chasing me."

"Who?"

"I don't know. But every time I go by there, it seems like the place tries to get my attention."

"What you mean?"

"It makes noises. And I thought I saw a light through that window over there," Jamie said, pointing. "I'm sure it was just my imagination. You know, because of the dreams."

"Interesting." Chris said. "What do you say we take a look?"

Jamie pulled back, his eyes wide. "What? You mean go in there?"

"No, silly. Let's just see if we can look through a window." Chris turned and trotted toward Vanderzee's. "C'mon, it'll be fine!" he yelled, beckoning Jamie with a wave of his hand.

"Famous last words," Jamie muttered as he watched Chris disappear around the side of the building. He hesitated, then ran to catch up, thinking, *I must be out of my mind.*

"Look! Up there! The board is falling off!" Chris yelled, pointing to a window high above their heads. He looked around the yard. "Over there, under the tree! That old crate should do the trick."

Together the boys dragged the crate until it rested beneath the window. Chris gave Jamie a boost up; then Jamie extended his hand and pulled Chris up too. Jamie tugged at the loose board. The rotted wood splintered and broke away, revealing a window with a broken latch and a filthy windowpane that looked as though someone had punched a fist through it.

Excited, Chris whispered, "I think someone's broken in here!"

Together the boys pushed the window upward until they had just enough room to poke their heads inside. Chris asked, "What's that over in the corner?"

Jamie squinted. "It looks like a pile of rags."

"Hmmmmm. Looks to me like a bed roll. I think someone has been sleeping in here. Probably hoboes."

Jamie said, "I don't think it could be very warm in there. In my dreams it was freezing!"

"No, I suppose not." Chris leaned his head further through the window and sniffed. "It smells smoky. Maybe that flickering light you saw was a fire someone built to keep warm."

"That makes sense," Jamie agreed. Just then, the church bells chimed.

CHAPTER 22

"Jeepers," said Chris, "It's five o'clock. We better get going."

In that instant, the sun set, plunging the boys into darkness in the shadow of Vanderzee's cold stone walls. Jamie shivered and leapt off the crate. Chris scrambled down too, and the boys took off like rabbits with a fox at their heels. Panting, they skidded to a stop when they reached the toboggan.

"Whew!" Jamie gasped for breath. "That place is bad enough during the day, but it really gives me the creeps in the dark!"

"I'll say!" Chris picked up the ropes to his toboggan and eyed the steep incline leading home. He sighed and said, "It's so much easier coming down than going up." Then he straightened up like a soldier about to begin a long march. "Well, here I go! See you tomorrow, Jamie."

"Okay, Chris. And thanks for showing me around Canterbury." Jamie watched Christopher start up the hill, his toboggan bouncing behind him. Then he turned and sprinted for Ida's like he was going for a record in the hundred yard dash.

CHAPTER 23

"Let's see if we can find some Christmas music on the wireless," Ida said. She was wearing her green and white gingham apron with embroidered red poinsettias dancing gaily on the pockets. She turned a brass knob on a dome-shaped Philco radio that sat atop a mahogany sideboard. Rusty, Fred, Roy and Big Ed were playing cards at a table they had set up in the middle of the parlor, and Jamie lay on his side on the floor, gazing with a blank stare at the fire in the hearth. The smell of the pork sausages and fried potatoes they'd had for supper lingered in the air.

The Christmas tree now stood between two frosty parlor windows that overlooked the porch. They had all made paper ornaments with their names printed in glitter and glue, and Jamie and Ida had strung garlands of popcorn and cranberries. Jamie thought the tree looked just as beautiful as the one in Grandma's living room, even without lights or tinsel.

"See if you can find Jack Benny," said Fred, "I love Jack Benny."

"Or Fred Allen," Roy chimed in. "I like his new show — what's it called — The Bath Tub Revue?"

"Linit Bath Club Revue," said Rusty, laughing. "Me, I like George Burns and Gracie Allen. That Gracie's a hoot."

"Yeah, she's dumb like a fox," Big Ed agreed. Static sputtered as Ida turned the radio dials. Suddenly, a tenor's voice burst through the radio. Jamie was only half listening until he heard the man sing, "Brother, can you spare a dime?" He sat up and listened hard as the singer's voice warbled on about building a railroad and making it run, followed again by that line, "Brother can you spare a dime?" Jamie felt his arm hairs stand on end.

"I think that's Al Jolson," Ida said.

"Yup, that's Jolson all right," Rusty confirmed. "He's got that distinctive warble in his voice."

Jamie said, "When we were in the village today, a raggedy-looking man asked us for a dime so he could eat. Christopher gave him a dime and his scarf. And a candy cane."

Rusty looked over the hand of cards fanned in front of his face. "That Christopher is a good fellow."

Roy said, "I've heard that in New York City, they line up on the sidewalks for miles just to get bread."

"I guess I didn't realize how bad the Depression was," Jamie said, bowing his head and feeling ashamed for having been afraid of the man who had asked them for a dime.

"It's easy to forget how lucky we are, living in this pretty town, practically in the lap of luxury here at Ida's, with a roof over our heads, a warm bed to sleep in and the finest home-cooking in a hundred miles," Rusty said. "But it's hard times out there for a lot of folks."

"True words," Fred agreed. "True words."

"Only a hundred miles?" Ida asked, and they all laughed. The song reached a crescendo and ended with the dramatic plea, "Brother, can you spaaaaaare … aaaaaaa …diiiiiiiii-ime?" The radio went silent, but for a moment the words hovered in the air. Seconds later, a snappy rendition of *Jingle Bells* burst through the radio, instantly changing the mood.

"Gin," said Big Ed, and the other men groaned as he laid out his hand and raked in the pot consisting of a few hard candies, a matchbook and bottle cap.

Jamie suddenly wanted to be alone. He got up, grabbed his jacket from the coat rack by the front door and slipped outside. An almost-full moon lit up the snowy landscape. Wisps of wood smoke from chimneys throughout the village floated like gray ghosts across the clear night sky.

Jamie sat down on the top step. He closed his eyes and let his mind wander. He remembered what Rusty had said the other night about hard times showing what people are made of. He thought about the man who had asked them for a dime and about people standing in lines to get bread. He thought about Christopher's generosity and about the kindness he'd been shown by the people of Canterbury.

Then his thoughts turned to his father. He had begun to understand how his dad might have felt when things went wrong – just like Jamie felt now, scared and not knowing what to do. Jamie thought about his mother, and for the first time, he realized how awful it must have been for her when his dad left, and how hard she had tried to protect him from what had happened. He longed for the sound of her voice and for the chance to rest his head in her lap again.

Jamie looked up at the moon. "I want to go home," he whispered, "I want to go home so much." His lower lip quivered. The muscles in his face began to twitch. His body trembled. The first sob was like a hiccup. The second one jerked his head and shoulders. The next one started as a wave in his belly that surged into his chest and flooded his heart with tears. Then wave after wave of sorrow pulsed through him, his whole body shuddering and tears gushing out like water from a geyser.

He wept for his father, who had lacked courage in a time of trouble, for his mother, who had tried to pick up the pieces, and for himself, for being caught in the middle of it all. He wept with frustration for the unfairness of being twelve years old and trying to solve a problem that seemed impossible. He wept with desperation for being far from home and with terror that he would never find his way back. He wept at the thought of never seeing his parents and grandparents again. He wept because he felt like time was running out.

After a long, long time, his sobs ebbed, until they were no longer waves but only ripples. Jamie wiped away his tears with a sleeve. Looking up, he saw a million stars twinkling in the clear night sky. He whispered, "Star light, star bright, first star I see tonight …." He stopped, feeling silly for reciting a little kid's poem about wishing on a star. *Well why not? I wished that I could come here and that happened, so why can't I wish to go back home?* He squeezed his eyelids shut and finished, "I wish I may, I wish I might … be home for Christmas."

The front door opened and Rusty stepped onto the porch. He buttoned his coat and turned the collar up around his ears. "Mind a little company? That Christmas music gets on my nerves after a while."

Jamie quickly wiped his eyes and breathed deeply. He wanted to say, "If you think that's bad, where I come from they start playing Christmas music the day after Halloween," but he just said, "I know what you mean."

Rusty sat down on the stoop. "You can see all the way to heaven on a night like this." Jamie kept his face turned away and didn't answer. Rusty put an arm around Jamie's shoulders. "I know it's hard to be away from family, especially at Christmas time."

Jamie said, "I'm scared that I'll never get back home. I miss my mom." He paused. "And I miss my dad, too," he added, surprising himself. "I tried to hate him for leaving us, but I miss him so much. I can't help it."

Rusty squeezed Jamie's shoulder and asked, "If you could talk to him right now, what would you say?"

Jamie thought for a moment. "I'd tell him that I'm really mad at him for messing up our lives, but that I think maybe I understand why he felt like he had to run away. I'd tell him that it really hurt Mom and me a lot and it's awful hard to stop being mad about it. And then I'd tell him that somehow – I don't know how, but somehow – everything will be all right." He rested his head on Rusty's sturdy shoulder and gazed up at the stars and the moon that shone down on them like sympathetic friends.

"That's right son," said Rusty. "One way or another, things will work out. They always do."

CHAPTER 24

When Jamie's eyes flew open the next morning, his first thought was, *I have to get home today!* He took long, deep breaths to calm the panic rising in his chest. Silently he prayed, *please help me figure out how to get home. Please.*

The seed of a plan had been growing in the back of his mind since yesterday. He had no idea if it would work, but having a plan felt better than not having one. He knew that he had to tell Kelly and Christopher the truth today. They might not believe him, but he needed their help. And, if he did succeed in getting back home, he wanted to be sure that his friends understood why he had suddenly disappeared.

After breakfast, Jamie bundled up for the cold uphill trek to the Pennysworth house. Ida watched him pull on his rugged L.L. Bean boots while she washed dishes in the sink. "You seem like your mind's a thousand miles away this mornin'," she said, drying her hands on her apron. "Anythin' you want to talk about?"

Jamie buttoned his jacket and pulled the wool cap over his ears. "It's just that I want so much to be home for Christmas, but I don't know if that's going to happen." His voice cracked and his bottom lip quivered. "But if I do get home, I'll miss you an awful lot."

Ida wrapped her plump arms around Jamie and drew him close. She smelled like vanilla and nutmeg, and Jamie knew that those would remain two of his favorite smells for as long as he lived. After a moment Ida let go and looked at him with moist emerald eyes. "If you do get home for Christmas – and I feel sure you will, you'll come back and see us sometimes, won't you?" Her voice trembled.

Jamie wiped a tear from his cheek and said, "Sure, you bet. And Miss Ida? If there isn't time later, I just want to say thank you. For everything."

Ida hugged him again, this time squeezing the breath out of him. "You're welcome, Jamie. But it's us that have you to thank for savin' Kelly and bringin' some youthful energy to our home." She held him away and cocked her head. "And why, pray tell, wouldn't there be time later?"

"I don't know," Jamie answered, shrugging. "I just wanted to say thanks – just in case. Anyway, I guess I better get going."

On his way out the door, Ida called, "Don't forget, we're havin' an early supper. We've got lots to do before the tree lightin' tonight. I'll need help frostin' the cookies and wrappin' the gifts."

"I won't forget," Jamie called over his shoulder. *I promise,* he thought, blinking back tears, *if I get back home … no,* when *I get home, I promise I'll never, ever, ever forget.*

CHAPTER 25

"Are you sad?" Kelly asked. "You sure look sad."

"Yeah, I am," Jamie answered. "I want to get home for Christmas, and I still really don't know how."

"Or where," Chris added.

"That's … not exactly true," Jamie said, avoiding their eyes.

"What do you mean?" Kelly asked. Then her eyes widened. She shouted, "I know! You've remembered something! I bet it's about Bell's Crossing right? You got all excited when we mentioned Bell's Crossing." She pounded Chris' arm with her fist and yelled, "Chris! I bet he lives in Bell's Crossing! Jamie, it's not far! Father could drive you there in the Ford!"

Jamie smiled sadly and said, "It's not quite that simple."

"Why not?" she asked, deflated.

Jamie inhaled deeply and blew out his breath. *You can't do this alone. You need to ask for help.* "I have something to tell you, but you're probably going to think I'm crazy. I'm not, but I wouldn't blame you if you think I am."

Kelly sat up straighter, eager to hear what he had to say. "Tell us. We promise to believe you."

"Yes, please tell us," Chris said.

Jamie said, "I never really lost my memory. I've always known where home is. And yes, I live in Bell's Crossing. Or at least that's where I was before I came here. Mom and I went there to spend Christmas with my grandparents."

"What about your father?" Kelly asked cautiously.

"My dad left us about a month ago." Jamie told them about the trouble his dad had gotten into, and how they left Hardcastle to get away from the scandal.

"I'm sorry, Jamie. That's awful," Kelly said.

"Yeah, tough luck," Chris added.

"Well, it's not as bad as what you guys have been through. With your mom I mean."

Chris lowered his eyes. Kelly bit her bottom lip and nodded. Jamie saw tears in her blue eyes. He quickly went on. "Things were cool in Bell's Crossing until I heard some women talking about us and I realized we hadn't escaped after all."

Jamie fidgeted. "Now here's where things start to get weird. My grandmother has a village of miniature cottages that she puts out at Christmas time. She calls it her Christmas Village. The name of the village is Canterbury."

Kelly drew back in surprise. "Your grandmother has a model of our town? I didn't know there was such a thing, did you, Chris?" Christopher shook his head.

"Everything is there – the church, the pine tree, your father's bank, the General Store, Ida's. And Vanderzee's too. Even *your* house."

Kelly clapped her hands. "Chris! Someone made a model of our house! Oh Jamie, I want to see it!"

Chris said. "That is pretty neat. I'm surprised I've never seen one of these villages. You'd think we would have heard about them. "

"The ice pond is there too. It's a mirror actually. And there are two skaters on it. A boy and a girl. And ... and ...."

"And what, Jamie?" Kelly leaned forward, her eyes bright.

"And ... *the skaters look exactly like you and Chris.*"

CHAPTER 26

"All right now, that *is* strange," Chris said, exchanging glances with Kelly.

"Hold on, there's more!" Jamie said. "Remember the other day when Iris said your father was going to Bell's Crossing and I went all weird on you?" Kelly and Chris nodded in unison. "And remember how I seemed surprised to find out that Canterbury was a real place?"

"That's right!" Kelly cried. "That *was* strange. I kept trying to figure out why you thought you were in a place that wasn't real."

"Well, there I was in the living room at Grandma and Grandpa's house. It was the night before Christmas Eve, and I was really sad. I kept thinking how pretty and peaceful the Christmas Village looked and how much I wished I could live there."

"But Jamie, the night before Christmas Eve was *last night*, and you were already *here* then," Kelly reminded him.

Jamie held up a palm. "I know, but stay with me. That night – the night before Christmas Eve – I fell asleep on the living room couch. The clock started chiming and woke me up. It was midnight. Then I heard laughter coming from somewhere in the room. I went over to look at the Christmas Village. And ... and...

"And what, Jamie? Go on! You're killing us!" Chris cried.

" ... And suddenly the skaters started throwing snowballs at each other."

Christopher shifted uncomfortably. Kelly's eyebrows knitted together in confusion. "So, wait a minute," she said slowly, "you mean the make-believe skaters in the make-believe village ... *came to life?*"

"*Yes.* I saw the boy throw a snowball at the girl and the girl chase after him. I saw the ice crack and give way under the girl's feet. And then I saw her fall through the ice into the pond."

Chris and Kelly's eyes widened. They listened spellbound as Jamie continued. "Kelly, I heard you scream for help. I saw Chris try to save you. You went down three times and when you came up the third time, you stretched your hand toward the sky as though you knew someone was up there watching. That's when I reached out like this ...." Jamie demonstrated his index finger-and-thumb rescue technique, "thinking I would just pluck you out and place you on the snow beside the pond. But the instant my fingers touched your hand, you pulled me into the Christmas Village."

Chris pursed his lips and said, "So, you mean to say that you were watching us, like ... like ... like ... as if we were watching people in Kelly's snow globe over there?"

"*Yes.* I know that sounds crazy but, it was *just* like that."

Chris frowned and shook his head. "I don't know, Jamie …."

"Chris! We promised to believe him!" Kelly cried, slapping Christopher's arm. She looked at Jamie with sincere eyes. "I believe you, Jamie. I do."

"Thanks, Kelly. But there's one more thing I have to tell you. It's the most important part, and it's the reason that getting me back to Bell's Crossing isn't as simple as having your father drive me there. When Kelly pulled me into Canterbury, the clock was chiming midnight and it was just turning Christmas Eve." Jamie took a deep breath, swallowed hard and said, "But it was Christmas Eve, *2007*."

cVo

CHAPTER 27

For a moment, the room was as so quiet that Jamie could hear himself breathe. He waited. Kelly's eyebrows knitted together and she wrinkled her nose. Then she grinned. "I knew it! I knew it!" she cried, clapping her hands. "You're from the future. I knew there was something different about your clothes and the way you talk." She turned to Chris. "Now it all makes sense!"

"What do mean it makes sense?" Chris cried. "It doesn't make any sense WHAT-SO-EVER!"

"Yes it does, silly! Remember how you never saw Jamie dive into the water, but *POOF!* Suddenly there he was, helping me get out. This explains *everything.*"

"Wait a minute," said Chris, exasperated. "Let's think about this logically. There's no such thing as time travel."

Jamie said, "I'm afraid I'm living proof that there is."

"Oh Jamie, this is so exciting!" Kelly cried. "Tell us, what is it like in 2007? You aren't speaking Russian or Chinese, so I guess this is still America. Are there rocket ships and men on the moon? Will the Depression end? Who am I going to marry? No! Wait! Don't tell me that. I want it to be a surprise."

Jamie laughed and said, "Slow down, slow down. Just because I'm from the future, that doesn't mean I'm psychic." He thought for a moment. He didn't want to overwhelm them by telling them things about the future that, though absolutely true, would nevertheless seem unbelievable. At last he said, "The Depression will last a while longer, but eventually it *will* end. And *yes*, there are rocket ships! The first astronaut will walk on the moon in 1969. His name is Neil Armstrong."

"What else?" Kelly leaned forward, her blue eyes gleaming. "It's like something out of an H.G. Wells or Jules Verne book. Chris, you're always telling me how much you love their science fiction stories."

"I love science fiction too," said Jamie. "In fact, I was just finishing *From Time to Time* by C.P. Franklin before I came here."

"What's it about?" Chris asked.

Jamie hesitated. He wrinkled his nose, lowered his eyes and said, "Time travel."

"Well there!" Chris thrust his arms in the air as if declaring victory. "It's probably all just power of suggestion. Jamie, don't you think that maybe you're still just confused about what's real and what isn't?"

Jamie shook his head. "I know I can't convince you, but it's NOT my imagination. It's definitely real. And it turns out that a lot of things that those guys wrote about actually came true, like submarines and scuba equipment and rocket boosters. One day soon, there will be something called television, which is like having movies coming through a box in your house. And people will walk around talking on telephones that fit in their pockets.

Chris guffawed. "Okay, now *that's* impossible! Kelly, can you just picture us all walking down the streets, talking on telephones, tripping over the cords?"

Jamie explained, "These phones don't need cords. They work with signals that travel through the air – like the wireless radio."

Chris pursed his lips and furrowed his brow. "Look, I want to believe you, but ...." His voice trailed off.

Kelly waved her hand dismissively. "Never mind him. What else Jamie? What about Bell's Crossing? Is it still a nice little town? Is the General Store still there?"

"Yes, and yes." Jamie said.

"I've been to the Bell's Crossing General Store!"

"I was there just a few days ago – seventy-five years from now." Jamie and Kelly beamed at each other, marveling at the wonder of it.

Chris snapped his fingers and shouted, "I know! I've got a question that will prove if what you're saying is true."

"Okay, shoot," Jamie said.

"All right, here it is: Will the Red Sox ever win another World Series?"

Jamie winced. "I hate to have to tell you this, Chris, but it's going to a very, very, very, *very* long wait."

Christopher's shoulders sagged and his chin dropped to his chest. "I was afraid you would say that." Then he lifted his face and broke into a huge grin. "But the good news is that you've finally said something I can actually believe."

"*Finally!*" Kelly cried, rolling her eyes and collapsing against her pillows.

"I could tell you lots of things about the future, but I don't want to take away the surprises," Jamie said. "But I do need to talk to you about my plan for getting back home. I'm *sure* that I have to go tonight."

"Why tonight?" Kelly asked.

"Because every day that I've been here, Canterbury has changed so that it looks more and more like Grandma's Christmas Village. Things like the lights getting put on the tree and the red bows on the lampposts. And in Grandma's village, there is a snowman down by the pond. Yesterday I helped two boys build that snowman. Oh! And the moon was full the night I left Bell's Crossing, and it's going to be full again tonight. And because it's Christmas Eve."

"I think I understand what you're saying," Chris said, getting the picture at last. "It's like the present – to you, the past, and the future – to you, the present, are starting to line up."

Kelly giggled. "Believe it or not, Chris, I actually understood what you just said!"

Jamie said, "Yes, that's it exactly! I think that by tonight, everything will be just right, and that's when I have to go."

"What are you going to do?" Kelly asked.

Jamie frowned. "*Well* ... I suppose it's not much of a plan, but I need to be out on the ice when the clock chimes midnight. I don't know how any of this works, but I think that you two need to be there too. You can't be out skating on the ice like you are in Grandma's village, but I still feel like you are supposed to be at the pond with me—do you think you can do that?"

"Of course. That makes perfect sense," Kelly said quickly. "We'll be there on the common anyway. We'll just slip away while everyone is singing carols."

Jamie said, "I'm hoping that there will be a sign, something that will show me what to do next. If not, then I guess I'm going to jump back into the hole in the ice and hope for the best."

"What can we do to help once we're there?" Chris asked.

Jamie looked at his friends' earnest faces. "I just need you to be there with me, to believe me, and to help me do whatever I have to do."

"We'll be there Jamie. Whatever it takes, we'll do it," Kelly said.

"You can count on us," Chris agreed, and reached out to shake Jamie's hand.

"Thanks, Chris. Thanks, Kelly. You two are the best friends I could ever have."

Kelly pulled open a drawer in her night table and took out a gold chain with a medallion dangling from the end. "Here, you may need this." She handed the chain to Jamie.

"What is it?"

"It's a St. Jude's medal."

"What's it for?"

"St. Jude is the patron saint of lost causes," Chris said.

Kelly rolled her eyes and slapped Chris's arm again. "Honestly, Chris, where are your brains? Don't listen to him Jamie. St. Jude is the saint who helps people find what they've lost."

Jamie pulled the chain over his head and rubbed the medallion between his fingers. "Thanks. I sure hope it's not a lost cause, but I'll definitely take all the help I can get."

CHAPTER 28

"On the first day of Christmas, my true love gave to meeeee," a voice sang out from the radio.

"A partri-idge in a pear treeeeee!" Ida's sweet soprano voice trilled from the kitchen.

"On the second day of Christmas, my true love gave to meeee ...." sang the radio.

"Two turtle doves," Rusty bellowed in his hearty baritone.

"And a partri-idge in a pear tree," repeated Ida, now joining Rusty, Jamie and the rest of the men gathered in the parlor. Fred took the next verse, followed by Roy. When they reached the fifth verse, Rusty pointed to Jamie, who blurted out, "FIVE GO-OLD RINGS!" and burst into laughter. Big Ed and Little Ed harmonized on "six geese a laying" and "seven swans a swimming," and the burly Harry leapt around the room while singing "eight Lords a leaping," in a high tenor voice that was so clear and pure, Jamie's jaw dropped in surprise.

When Ida took another turn singing, "nine ladies dancing," Rusty grabbed her by the waist and twirled her around the room. Ida's cheeks flushed crimson and she tried to wriggle free, but her green eyes sparkled and she looked happy. Everyone chimed in for the final chorus, fairly shaking the shingles off the roof as they sang, "And a partri-idge in a peeeeeeaaaaarrrrr treeeeeeeeee!" each in his own key.

Jamie collapsed on the floor in a fit of laughter and exhaustion. He gazed around the room, filling his eyes with the happy scene – the fire in the hearth, the tree with its simple decorations, the soft candlelight casting a glow over each smiling face. He closed his eyes, imprinting the images in his mind. He inhaled the scent of pine, the pleasant smokiness of the fire and the mingled aromas of chicken pot pie, homemade bread and apple dumplings.

After supper, Jamie went upstairs to change clothes. He opened the top bureau drawer and dug beneath the clothes Chris had given him to find the ones he had been wearing the night he came to Canterbury. He stepped into his navy blue corduroys, buttoned his red and green flannel shirt and pulled on his socks.

Jamie sat down on the bed and touched the St. Jude medallion that hung around his neck. He tucked it securely inside his shirt, closed his eyes and felt a strange sense of calm settle in. He took a deep breath, opened his eyes and said, "It's time to go."

CHAPTER 29

By nine o'clock, a good-sized crowd had gathered on the common where the giant pine tree patiently awaited its moment of glory. A bonfire raged in a pit a safe distance away, and the Altar Guild Ladies had set up their tables close by. A man dressed as Santa Claus cheerfully accepted wrapped gifts and deposited them into a red sleigh.

Jamie helped Ida unpack a basket she had filled with pies and the star-shaped Christmas cookies he had helped her decorate that afternoon with white icing and red and green sprinkles. Their goodies joined the endless array of home-made cranberry-nut breads, muffins, frosted cupcakes and a few dreadful-looking fruit cakes.

Hundreds of candles lined the sidewalk leading to the church. Children played games and napped in the church hall while they waited for eleven o'clock, when the tree lights would finally be turned on. The organist pounded out Christmas music that poured out the open church doors and skated through the thin night air.

Jamie watched families arrive, wearing layers of warm clothing and bright smiles. He watched them greet neighbors and friends with hugs and shouts of "Merry Christmas!" Fighting waves of sadness and envy, he shoved his hands deep in his pockets and turned to look at the pond. The full moon reflected off the ice like a mirror. Although he had expected it, Jamie's heart still skipped a beat when he saw that the snowman now sported a black top hat and a bright orange scarf with a large black "P" on one end.

"Jamie! Over here! Jamie!"

He turned to see an elegant black sleigh drawn by a team of sleek black horses. Mr. Pennysworth held the reins, and Kelly sat beside him, waving at Jamie and calling to him. Chris sat in the back seat beside Iris Gordon, who was holding Emilie in her arms.

Jamie ran to greet them. "Is this your sleigh?" he asked, extending a hand to Kelly.

"Yes! Isn't it lovely?" Jamie noticed Kelly's rosy cheeks and the sparkle in her blue eyes. She looked healthy and fully recovered from her near-drowning experience. She was dressed for the holiday in a bright red wool coat with a black velvet collar. Her blond hair had been curled into waves that hung almost to her waist, and on her head she wore a red stocking hat with a white pompom.

Kelly hopped down and hugged him. "Merry Christmas, Jamie." She reached into her pocket and pulled out another hat just like hers. "Here, I brought one for you."

Jamie pulled off his scratchy gray wool cap and replaced it with the stocking cap. "Thanks! How do I look?"

"Like a very excellent Santa's helper!" Kelly said, adjusting it to a jauntier angle.

"Merry Christmas, Jamie," Mr. Pennysworth said, jumping down from the sleigh.

"Merry Christmas, Jamie!" Iris and Chris called.

"Merry Christmas, Mr. Pennysworth! Merry Christmas, Mrs. Gordon! Merry Christmas, Chris!" Jamie called back. In spite of his jitters about the night ahead, in that moment Jamie felt like it was truly a Merry Christmas Eve.

"Jamie, will you hold Emilie while I step down?" Iris asked. "You remember how, don't you?"

"Sure!" Jamie took the baby and held her the way Iris had shown him.

Emilie's soft brown eyes gazed at him as though she recognized him. She grinned, revealing the impressive dimple in her left cheek, and said, "Goo!"

"Goo to you too!" Jamie laughed and bounced Emilie in his arms. Mr. Pennysworth helped Iris from the sleigh and lifted out the baby's carriage. Jamie placed Emilie inside and Iris tucked a fuzzy white blanket over her. "There, sweet pea," Iris crooned, "you should be as snug as a bug in a rug!"

"What was that?" Jamie shrieked, hopping from one foot to the other as though dancing an Irish jig. A small black dog with a red plaid bow around its neck scampered between his legs, almost knocking him down. The dog sprinted across the street and raced around in the snow, darting this way and that way. Suddenly the dog stopped, tilted its head and studied the snowman that stood mutely nearby. Slowly and cautiously, the dog approached the snowman and sniffed at it. Jamie's heart lurched. Grandma's Christmas Village scene was nearly complete now, right down to the snowman-sniffing dog. He knew that soon the carolers would assemble beneath the tree, song books in hand. The final pieces were falling into place, but Jamie still didn't quite know what to do with them.

Christopher and Kelly came and stood beside him. Chris laid a hand on Jamie's shoulder. Kelly took Jamie's hand and squeezed it. For a moment the three friends gazed silently at the pond and watched the dog until it lost interest in the snowman and ran off down Main Street. The church bells chimed ten o'clock. At last Chris said, "Aunt Polly brought warm doughnuts from her restaurant. Let's go get one."

Jamie chose a sticky honey-glazed doughnut that was so airy and sweet; it made his eyes roll back in his head. He licked the honey from his fingers and washed it down with hot, cinnamon-spiked cider.

At ten thirty, a group of men, women and children wearing Victorian clothing gathered in a semi-circle beneath the tree. Doc Fernald appeared, wearing a black tuxedo with long tails, a black top hat and a red and white striped scarf. He set up a music stand in front of the carolers and laid out his music sheets. He tapped a conductor's baton three times and raised his arms. The carolers opened their song books, straightened their posture, and when Doc swung his arms downward and out with a dramatic flourish, they began to sing *Good King Wenceslas*.

The crowd joined in, singing with gusto. Jamie spotted the man who had asked for a dime standing across the way, wearing the scarf Chris had given him and singing with all his heart. The man saw Jamie, smiled a lopsided grin and flipped the tail of his scarf over his shoulder. Jamie grinned back and for some reason, saluted. The man instantly straightened up and returned the salute with the flourish of a seasoned soldier.

Kelly cried, "Look it's snowing!" and indeed it was. Giant snowflakes landed weightlessly on their heads and shoulders. Jamie turned his face to the sky and stuck out his tongue, catching the flakes as they fell.

Just before eleven, the carolers burst into a rousing chorus of *We Wish You a Merry Christmas*. Jamie scanned the faces in the crowd. He felt a tug on his heart. There was Rusty with his arm protectively around Ida's waist, and this time she wasn't shooing him away. There were Big Ed and Little Ed, harmonizing on the chorus. There was Mr. Pennysworth, with Iris Gordon beside him, Emilie's baby carriage tucked close by her side.

In that millisecond of stillness after the song ended, the tree lit up, washing golden light over all their faces. The crowd gasped and cheered. Everyone hugged and shouted, "Merry Christmas!" Jamie spotted Jake and Rodney on the street corner near the electrical box, jumping up and down and hugging.

Christopher hugged Kelly and they both hugged Jamie. "Merry Christmas, Jamie," Kelly said.

"Merry Christmas, Kelly. Merry Christmas, Christopher." At that moment, the church bells began to chime and the crowd hushed. *Eleven o'clock.* A shiver ran up Jamie's spine. *Just one more hour.* Jamie closed his eyes and prayed, *please,*

please, please help me get back home. The last chime rang out. For a heartbeat or two, the only sound was the echo of the bells hovering over the common, skimming across the pond and disappearing down the empty streets of Canterbury.

Then a blood-chilling scream ripped through the peaceful night, shattering the silence like breaking glass.

CHAPTER 30

Everything seemed to happen in slow motion. All heads turned to see Iris Gordon bending over the baby carriage, hands to her cheeks, screaming again and again and again. She collapsed against Mr. Pennysworth, sobbing. Jamie saw a piece of paper slip from her hand and flutter to the ground. Rusty picked it up, and he and Ida read it silently.

Then everything happened at the speed of light. The crowd converged around Iris and Mr. Pennysworth. Jamie, Kelly and Chris sprinted across the common and pushed their way through, ducking under elbows and squeezing between legs. "Father! What's happened?" Christopher asked. Mr. Pennysworth's face looked pale and he held tightly to Iris, who seemed like she would crumple to the ground without his support.

Kelly peered into the baby carriage. She picked up the baby. "Why, it's just a doll!" she cried, her eyes wide and her expression a combination of wonder and confusion. "What's happened, Father? Where's Emilie?"

Iris pushed away from Mr. Pennysworth and looked at him with terrified eyes. Tears streamed down her face. Between choking sobs she said, "It's Jim. He's taken Emilie. Oh, this is all my fault!" Iris trembled from head to toe. "He wanted me to steal from you, but I couldn't do it! You've been so good to us. I didn't think he would really do anything. This is all my fault, all my fault." She collapsed against Mr. Pennysworth's chest, dissolving into tears.

Rusty said, "The note says that he wants a thousand dollars by midnight. You're supposed to put the money in a bag and hang it from the tree. Once he has the money, he'll leave a note in the Santa sleigh, telling us where to find Emilie."

Mr. Pennysworth comforted Iris. "This is *not* your fault. We'll find Emilie, I promise we will. I'll go to the bank right now and take the money out of my own account. Ida, please take Iris up to the church. See if you can find some brandy or wine to calm her nerves."

Ida put her arm around Iris' shoulders and helped her up the hill.

Rusty said, "I'll organize search parties."

Mr. Pennysworth nodded and shook Rusty's hand. "Good idea, thanks."

Chris stepped forward. "Father, we want to help too!"

"*NO!*" Mr. Pennysworth bellowed, his tone so sharp that it made Jamie jump. Mr. Pennysworth took a deep breath. Placing a firm hand on Chris' shoulder he said, "No, son, it's too late, too dark, too cold and too dangerous. I need you to take care of your sister. She can't stay out in the cold."

"But Father …!" Chris protested.

To Jamie's surprise, Kelly grabbed Christopher's arm. "It's all right, Chris. Let's go up to the church and get warm. I'm freezing!" She tipped her head toward the church and gave Chris a look that said, "Don't argue!"

Jamie watched Mr. Pennysworth run down Main Street, slipping and sliding in the half-inch of snow that had already fallen. Mothers gathered their children close and headed to the church. Rusty called out to the crowd for volunteers to search for the baby. At least a hundred people crowded around, eager to help.

Jamie glanced at the church clock. *Ten past eleven.* His heart skipped. There wasn't much time before he had to leave, and now Emilie was kidnapped! *Don't panic, don't panic.* He breathed deeply, trying to calm his frazzled nerves.

"All right, let's go to the church then," Chris said, resigned to their fate.

Kelly said, "Wait! I forgot something in the sleigh." She started walking, then turned and looked at the boys, hands on her hips. "Well, come on, you two, I need your help." Jamie and Chris exchanged glances, shrugged and followed.

Kelly climbed into the sleigh, still holding onto the doll she had taken from Emilie's carriage. Jamie and Chris clambered in after her. "So what did you forget?" Chris asked, surveying the bare seats.

Kelly rolled her eyes. "Nothing, silly! It was just a trick to get us away from there so we can figure out what to do. I'm *NOT* a sickly little girl and I'm *NOT* going to stay in the church when we should be helping to find Emilie!" Her back stiffened and she shot the boys another "don't-you-dare-argue-with-me" look.

Chris held up his hands as if to say "I surrender." Jamie nodded his silent agreement, though his heart felt sick with worry and fear. He wanted to get home more than anything in the world, and midnight was less than an hour away.

"So what's our plan?" Chris asked.

Just then, the hobo walked by, his shoulders hunched against the cold. "Excuse me, sir!" Jamie called.

"Hello, again, my young friendth," the man said.

"Hi! I'm Jamie. And this is Chris, and this is Kelly."

"Pleathed to meet you all. My name ith Reginald Van Dyke. But you can call me Reggie."

"Nice to meet you, Reggie. Do you mind if I ask you a question?"

"Athk away. But hurry, I want to thart looking for that poor little baby." He shook his head. "What a terrible, terrible thing. And on Chrithmuth Eve, too."

"Have you by any chance been staying over at Vanderzee's?"

Reggie shifted from foot to foot and pursed his lips.

Jamie quickly added, "It's all right. We promise we won't tell anyone. It's really important. A matter of life and death."

"Well ... in that cathe... I may have had occathon to thtay there onth or twithe."

Jamie leaned forward, his eyes bright with excitement. "Have you ever seen Jim Gordon there?"

Reggie nodded. "Yeah, I theen him over there a few timeth. Him and thum other fella. Theemed like they wath up to no good, tho I gave them a wide berth. But I haven't theen them there in a while, tho I figured they'd moved on."

Jamie looked at Chris, who nodded that he understood. "What's going on?" Kelly asked. "What's all this about Vanderzee's?"

"I'll explain in a second," Jamie said, his excitement building. "Reggie, we saw a broken window. Is that how you got in?"

"Nah. I've got a much better way. But thath no plathe for you kidth. Why do you want to get in there?

"It's just a hunch, but I think that might be where they've taken Emilie." Jamie knew that it could just be a coincidence, but his gut told him that he now knew the reason for his dreams about Vanderzee's and his strange connection with the place.

"Well ith worth a look, I gueth. I can thow you my way in, if you want."

"Climb up!" Jamie said, extending a hand.

Reggie grabbed it, then hesitated. "Thouldn't we go back and get thum grown-upth?"

Jamie cried, "We haven't got time!" His heart pounded. Every second they delayed now put Emilie – and his plans – further in jeopardy.

Reggie glanced toward the church. Jamie tugged Reggie's hand and said firmly, "We're going now, with or without you."

Looking back over her shoulder, Kelly added, "Reggie, you *are* a grown-up."

Reggie nodded, as though suddenly remembering something he had forgotten. He placed his foot on the runner and Jamie hauled him into the sleigh.

"Okay, Millie! Okay, Tillie! Let's go!" Kelly urged the horses. She snapped the reins and steered the sleigh down the middle of Main Street, keeping the horses to a slow pace so as not to call attention to themselves. Then she snapped the reins again, and the horses broke into a trot, the clip-clop of their hooves muffled by the new dusting of snow on the street.

Jamie glanced over his shoulder and saw the crowd breaking up. He looked up at the church clock. *Eleven-twenty*. His blood ran cold and his hands shook. Panic gripped him as he watched the pond grow smaller and smaller in the distance. One half of his brain screamed, *get off the sleigh, NOW!* The other half whispered, *Emilie needs your help*. The sleigh rounded a curve and the pond disappeared from sight. Jamie leaned forward, trembling from the crown of his head to the tips of his toes, and tapped Kelly's shoulder.

"What, Jamie?" she called, without looking back.

"Go faster, Kelly!" he shouted. "Go faster!"

CHAPTER 31

"Giddy-up!" Kelly yelled. The horses broke into a gallop. Jamie gripped the side of the sleigh as they raced down Main Street, past Aunt Polly's Kitchen and the Canterbury General Store. He saw lights in the bank as they whizzed past, and knew it must be Mr. Pennysworth getting the ransom money. Two minutes later, Vanderzee's Welding & Ironworks appeared ahead of them like a medieval castle surrounded by a moat of snow.

"Pull up behind those trees!" Jamie called, "We don't want them to hear us coming or see the sleigh!" Kelly reined in the horses and steered them into a cluster of pine trees. "Okay, Reggie, show us the way," Jamie said. "Sssshhhhhh, everyone, we need to be quiet from now on."

Reggie led them single-file around the back of the building. Jamie's heart hammered and his palms began to sweat inside his mittens. Reggie pointed to a shallow u-shaped well surrounding a basement window. He lowered himself down and lifted the window. He motioned for Jamie to follow.

Reggie pointed to the open window, indicating that Jamie should go inside. Jamie hesitated, then summoned his courage and crawled through. He stepped easily onto a crate and dropped to the floor. A moment later Chris joined him, followed by Kelly and Reggie.

Chris whispered, "What did you bring that doll for?"

"I don't know. I wasn't thinking. I'll just leave it here," Kelly said, placing the doll on the floor.

Reggie lit a match. In the time it took to burn out, Jamie saw that they were in a large, nearly empty basement with stone walls and floor. He caught the faint, familiar odor of metal and tasted rust in the air. Across the room, a flight of wooden stairs led up to a door. The match went out.

"Hold handth and follow me. Thtay together." They climbed slowly and quietly. Jamie brushed against a cobweb and recoiled, his heart beating like it would pop through his chest.

Reggie cracked open the door at the top of the stairs. A thin beam of light peeked through the slit, offering a glimpse into an office with old wooden desks, chairs and filing cabinets. No one was there, but they could hear low voices coming through a door across the room. Then, a baby cried. Kelly squeezed Jamie's hand so hard his knuckles hurt. *He'd been right! Emilie was here!*

"Can't you shut that baby up?" Jim yelled.

Footsteps scuffled across the floor. Emilie's cries stopped. A different voice said, "Thank God for pacifiers."

"All right, Pete," said Jim. "Here's the note tellin' them to look for the baby over at Fallon's Covered Bridge. You grab the money bag from the tree and put the note in the sleigh. Then get back here as fast as you can."

"How will we get the baby over to the bridge without being seen?" Pete asked.

"Don't be stupid! We're not takin' the baby anywhere. We just want to keep them chasin' their tails on the other side of town while we get out of here."

"What about the baby?"

"Don't worry about the baby," Jim growled. "Now get goin'."

Kelly squeezed Jamie's hand again. Jamie squeezed back, as if to say, "I don't like that sound of that either."

"Be back in a while," Pete said. They heard a window scrape open, more scuffling sounds, then silence.

The group descended the stairs and huddled together. Reggie lit another match. "I have an idea," Jamie said, and described the plan that had been forming in his mind since they got there. They whispered back and forth, filling in the gaps and nailing down the details.

"Wait!" Kelly whispered, picking up the doll, "I think this will come in handy after all."

"Good thinking!" said Chris with a smirk in his voice. "I'm glad I insisted that you bring it."

"Okay, then," Jamie said, "Reggie goes up first. Then Chris and I have to act fast." He turned to Kelly. "Kelly, you get back to the sleigh and have it ready to bolt the minute Chris gets there with Emilie, okay?"

"I'll be ready," Kelly said solemnly. She climbed onto the crate and crawled out the cellar window. A second later, she poked her head back inside. "Good luck everyone. Be careful! And Jamie, please hurry! There isn't much time until midnight."

"I know. I'll make it, don't worry." Jamie knew that in the darkness, the others couldn't see his face drained of color and the worried look in his eyes. But tiny Emilie was in danger right upstairs, and no matter what, he had to stay and see things through now. *No matter what.*

"All right, then," Kelly said, "I'll see you at the pond at midnight."

CHAPTER 32

"We with you a Merry Chrithmuth, We with you a Merry Chrithmuth...." Reggie burst through the door singing at the top of his lungs and slurring his words. Using the noise for cover, Jamie and Chris scurried in after him and hid behind a desk. They watched Reggie stagger across the room and weave through the second door.

"What the ....?" Jim shouted. Then, "Oh it's just you."

"And a Happy New Yeeeeeeaaaaarrr!" Reggie belted out the ending and threw his arms around Jim, pushing him away from the doorway and farther into the next room. Jamie and Chris flattened themselves on the floor and watched from beneath the desk.

"Hey old buddy old pal. Merry Chrithmuth," Reggie said, thumping Jim on the back. "I got you a Chrithmuth prethent." Reggie took out his candy cane and offered it to Jim.

Jim slapped the candy cane away with disgust. "Drunken fool," he muttered.

Jamie's heart raced as he spotted Emilie lying on blankets on the floor. He saw another door beyond her and drew in his breath. He knew in his gut what lay beyond that door.

Reggie broke into a chorus of *Jingle Bells,* their agreed-upon cue. Jamie picked up the doll and nodded to Chris. Quickly the boys scooted to the wall. Jamie peeked around the doorjamb and saw Reggie staggering around the room, still singing at the top of his lungs. Suddenly, Reggie stumbled into Jim and knocked him to the floor with Reggie landing on top.

Jim screamed, "IDIOT!" as the men wrestled, their arms and legs flailing like an octopus tangled in a fishing net. Reggie pretended to try to get up, but kept collapsing on Jim, all the while shouting, "Thorry! Tho clumthy of me!"

Chris and Jamie tiptoed into the room. Chris scooped up Emilie and bolted back through the office toward the stairs leading to the basement. Jamie quickly wrapped the doll in Emilie's blankets and ran across the room, leaping right over the two men wrangling on the floor.

"Hey! What's goin' on?" Jim yelled, suddenly realizing that someone else was there. Jamie stopped and locked eyes with him. "You again!" Jim screamed, his black eyes ablaze with fury.

Jamie turned so that Jim could see the decoy "baby" wrapped in blankets in his arms. As much as Jamie wanted to get out of there fast and get back to the pond, the plan was for him to keep Jim occupied so that Chris and Kelly could get Emilie to safety. Chris had argued that he should be the one to stay behind, but Jamie insisted that his dream had given him the advantage of knowing what to expect and how to escape. He had passionately stated his case, explaining that he knew in his heart that his strange connection with Vanderzee's had been for a reason, and that reason was to save Emilie now. In the end, they reluctantly agreed to let Jamie be the one to stay and distract Jim while they escaped with Emilie in the sleigh.

Jim yelled, "Hey! Hey! Hey!" and struggled harder to untangle himself from Reggie. But Reggie was surprisingly strong and managed to keep him pinned.

Swallowing hard, Jamie turned the knob on the door that he knew in his gut would lead him onto the dark, cold factory floor of Vanderzee's Welding & Ironworks. He stepped through and let it slam shut behind him. *Phase one complete,* he thought, his heart pumping.

He tried to get his bearings in the cavernous, pitch-black room. The outlines of hundreds of machines loomed like a herd of buffalo in the darkness. The familiar metallic smell was stronger now. Jamie shivered. The air felt as cold as the inside of a freezer. His heart roared like a freight train barreling through a tunnel. Everything was like it had been in his dreams, only now it was real.

Jim screamed, "Get off me, you drunken fool!" followed by more scuffling sounds beyond the door. Jamie took off, one arm holding the doll, one arm extended. He heard the factory door open and then bang shut, its tinny echo resonating everywhere.

"I know you're in here, boy," Jim shouted, his voice bouncing off the walls.

Good! Jim had followed him! Jamie huddled behind a machine, listening. His eyes searched the darkness for a glimpse of the door that he knew must be there, the one through which he would escape. *Where is it?* Jamie took a deep breath and ran. He slipped on metal shavings, then righted himself quickly. Suddenly he was yanked from behind by the collar of his coat. He fell backwards, let go of the doll and looked up to see Jim's toothy, white grin hovering in the darkness like a crescent moon in a midnight sky.

"Hello Jamie." Jamie could hear the sneer in Jim's voice. He wriggled out of his jacket, picked up the doll and sprinted. He dropped to the floor, rolled under a machine and kept rolling. He got up and ran. Suddenly his outstretched hand touched wood. *The wall!* He threw the doll aside and scooted sideways, frantically searching for the door that he hoped upon hope existed in reality and not just in his dreams. His fingers brushed metal. *The latch!* He jiggled it and pushed hard. *Nothing.* Jamie's heart pounded in his ears.

Jim's labored breath grew louder. *He's getting closer!* Jamie fumbled blindly for the slide lock. *There it is!* A surge of hope fueled him as he frantically tugged. *C'mon c'mon, c'mon!* The lock slid, then stuck. He yanked again. It slid, stuck and then jerked free. *Yes!*

Jamie shoved his weight against the door. It budged an inch and stuck. *Okay, okay. Breathe! You're almost there now!* Jamie took a deep breath, leaned back and rammed the door with his whole body.

CHAPTER 32

The rusty old hinges broke. The door burst open. Jamie sailed through it, landing face-first in a snow bank. He scrambled to his feet and ran like the devil was at his heels.

It had stopped snowing. The full moon lit the way. His boots crunched over the snow. His breath and his footsteps were the only sounds in the eerily silent night. He raced past the chestnut tree. As he passed the cluster of pines where they had hidden the sleigh, he leapt in the air with joy and burst into a smile as wide as the ocean. His mind screamed, *Yippee! The sleigh is gone! We did it!*

Jamie kicked into high gear, his feet barely touching the snowy ground. Wild euphoria fueled him as he raced down Main Street. *Emilie is safe! No matter what else happens now, my friends are safe!*

CHAPTER 33

Jamie felt like he was running through a dreamscape. Main Street was completely deserted. The bank looked dark again. He raced past the Canterbury General Store and Aunt Polly's Restaurant, each with gay wreaths on the doors and windows. Aunt Polly had posted a sign that read, "Free Dinner on Christmas Day." Looking down, Jamie saw hoof prints and sleigh tracks in the soft layer of snow. His heart soared and he picked up his pace. The red holiday bows on the lamp posts flapped in the wind like flags cheering him toward a finish line.

"Merry Christmas, Mr. Confederate Soldier!" Jamie yelled as he sped past the statue in the town square. He rounded a curve and the common burst into view. The huge pine was a glorious sight, lighting up his path like a runway. He glanced up at the church. No one was outside, but the sleigh was parked in front, the horses' backs covered with blankets. Jamie summoned his courage and raised his eyes to the clock. *Six minutes to twelve.*

I made it! His mind screamed with joy as he veered toward the pond. He saw the snowman keeping vigil, and just beyond, Kelly and Chris waiting for him. They saw him too and jumped up and down, waving their arms in the air.

"Jamie! Hurry!" Kelly shouted. "It's almost midnight!"

"You made it!" yelled Chris as Jamie skidded to a stop.

"There's not much time," Jamie said, bending over and panting. "But tell me quickly, what's happened?"

Kelly said, "It was amazing! Chris ran up holding Emilie and we flew down Main Street like Santa in his sleigh. She was so good, she didn't even cry. When we got to the church, everyone was shocked that we found her. Father would have been angry, but he was so relieved that Emilie was safe, he really couldn't be. Iris couldn't stop crying, she was so happy and relieved. Father and some of the others set out to bring back the search parties so they could all go down to Vanderzee's and arrest Jim."

Chris jumped in to finish the story. "In all the commotion, we forgot about the moneybag hanging on the tree. But Ida spotted Pete sneaking around down there, and before you knew it, the whole Ladies' Altar Guild swarmed down the hill like angry bees. They surrounded him and Mabel Bixby – you know, that really large lady with the red hair – wrestled him to the ground and sat on him until Officer Leahy got there. They've got him up in the church right now, under house arrest." Chris grinned. "Or church arrest, I guess."

Jamie sat on the ground, tugging off his boots. "What did you tell them about how we found Emilie?"

CHAPTER 33

"We said that you had a hunch about Vanderzee's and that when Reggie told us he'd seen Jim there, we decided to take a look. We told them how Reggie tricked Jim by pretending to be drunk and distracted him so we could get Emilie out of there."

"What happened at Vanderzee's?" Kelly asked. "Is Jim still there? Is Reggie all right? Where's your coat?"

"Reggie was exceptional! He kept Jim pinned down while Chris got away with Emilie. I made sure Jim saw me holding the baby – the doll – so that he would follow me like we planned. After that, everything was just like it was in my dreams – just like I knew it would be. Jim grabbed me by the collar. I wriggled out of my coat and ran. I found the door, and then poof! I was out and running down Main Street. When I saw the sleigh was gone, I knew that you had gotten away." Jamie noticed that Christopher was holding something. "Hey, what's that?"

Chris held up a burlap sack. "It's the money bag. We were in such a hurry to meet you here, I forgot I still had it."

Jamie glanced at the steeple clock. *Three minutes to twelve.* His face grew serious. "I've got to go." Kelly threw her arms around his neck. She started to shake and he knew that she was crying. Jamie's eyes welled up too. "Thank you for everything," he said, his voice barely above a croak.

"Thank *you*," Kelly said, releasing him. "If it weren't for you, I wouldn't even be here now. And who knows what would have happened to Emilie! You saved us both."

Chris and Jamie hugged next. "Thanks Jamie," said Chris. "We sure will miss you."

"I'll miss you too. Both of you. I'll miss everyone here more than you'll ever know." He stepped onto the ice in his stocking feet and slid a little way out. Despite the cold and having no coat or shoes, he felt oddly warm. "Well, I guess this is it. I don't know what's going to happen, but I sure hope something does." He slid further onto the ice.

"Look out, Chris!" Kelly shrieked. Jamie spun around. Jim appeared out of nowhere, crashing across the snow and lunging for the bag in Chris' hand. Chris managed to spin away and lob the bag high in the air. It flew over the ice and fell into Jamie's outstretched arms. When Jamie looked back again, he saw Chris lying on the ground and Jim holding Kelly roughly by the arm, a triumphant sneer on his face.

Bong.

CHAPTER 34

Midnight!

Jamie froze, stunned. *Time to go! NOW!!* He stared at Kelly and Jim, her face pale in the moonlight, his face flushed with rage.

"Give me that bag and I'll let her go," Jim shouted.

"Let her go and I'll give you the bag!" Jamie shouted back.

Bong.

"No! Jamie! Go! You've got to go!" Kelly screamed. "Don't worry about me! Just go!"

"Throw me the bag!" Jim's voice sounded high-pitched and strained. Even at this distance, Jamie could see the fury blazing like fire in Jim's eyes.

Bong.

Jamie dangled the bag enticingly. "Come and get it!" He glanced over his shoulder and saw that the hole was about twenty feet behind him. He inched backwards.

Jim stepped onto the ice, gripping Kelly's arm. She wriggled and tried to punch him with her free hand, but he held

161

her fast. He kept moving toward Jamie, dragging Kelly with him.

Bong.

Suddenly Jim's head jerked forward as though he had been hit from behind. For a split-second, it looked as though the back of his head had exploded in a puff of white powder. Then Jamie saw snowballs blazing through the air, and Chris winding up again and again and again. The next snowball caught Jim squarely on the right ear. He reeled around, instinctively raising his hand to his head and letting go of Kelly's arm. Seizing her chance, Kelly kicked him in the shin and ran to shore.

Bong.

Jim swiveled toward Chris, who was taking aim with another snowball, then back toward Jamie. Jamie held the money bag high, like a matador teasing a bull with his cape. "I've got what you want, Jim! Come and get it!"

Bong.

Jamie turned and ran toward the hole, slipping and sliding over the ice.

"Run, Jamie, Run!" Kelly screamed.

Bong.

Jim ran after him, snowballs whizzing past his head as Kelly joined Chris in the snowball assault.

Ten feet. Jamie heard Jim's panting breath and sensed him closing the gap.

Bong.

Eight feet, five feet, three feet. Jamie gathered speed and took a running leap up and over the hole in the ice. He tossed the money bag high in the air. In that very instant, time slowed down so that Jamie felt like he was floating through molasses. His movements, and everyone else's, seemed to be in slow motion, and sounds were muted and drawn out, like a recording played on slow speed.

Boooooong.

Jim stormed across the ice. The bag somersaulted through the air. Kelly and Chris jumped up and down on shore, waving their arms and screaming. A crowd streamed out of the church and down the hill.

Boooooong.

Jim leapt up, arms flailing as he grabbed for the bag. His hands closed around it and he grinned his sneering, victorious smile as he clutched it to his chest. Then he plummeted toward earth, his feet smashing against the thin layer of ice covering the hole. His expression quickly changed from glee to shock as the ice gave way and he crashed through it, plunging straight down into the frigid water, still clinging to his bag of money.

Boooooong.

Jim thrashed around, trying to hold onto the bag and stay afloat.

The crowd converged at the edge of the ice.

Boooooong.

Jamie felt himself drifting farther and farther and farther away. Everyone and everything seemed so small and distant, as though he were looking through the wrong end of binoculars. Voices were no more than faint whispers on the wind. The pond and the people below grew smaller and smaller and smaller, until Jamie could barely distinguish one person from another. His eyes homed in on one tiny figure, now no more than a speck of bright red, her tiny white- gloved hand waving and waving and waving at him until she disappeared, along with everything else below, into total darkness.

CHAPTER 35

*B*ong.

Jamie's exhausted mind tried to crawl back from a deep sleep.

Bong.

The church clock is still chiming, he thought. *NO!* his mind screamed, *I didn't make it! I didn't make it home!* His eyes flew open.

Bong.

It took a moment for Jamie's gaze to fully focus. He was lying on the floor. He pushed up onto one elbow.

Bong.

There was Grandma's green velvet couch.

Bong.

There was the quilt he'd left lying on the floor.

Bong.

There was the grandfather clock by the living room door, chiming six o'clock.

I'm home! I DID make it! I made it home for Christmas! His heart soared. *I'm home! I'm HOME! I'm HOME!!*

Jamie spun to look at the Christmas Village. Everything was just the way it had been before: the miniature cottages; the tiny carolers singing beneath the pine tree; the snowman with the top hat and the orange scarf standing guard beside the pond; the pocket-sized boy and girl skating on the pond. Still. Peaceful. *Inanimate.*

There was no crack in the mirror pond, no hole in the ice. No movement or sounds came from Ida's Boarding House. No shutters flapped in the wind at Vanderzee's Welding & Ironworks. *Was it real? Was it a dream? It was too real to be a dream!*

Jamie reached out and lightly touched the skaters with his fingertip. *It must have been a dream.* His eyes welled with tears. *No! It can't have been a dream, they were my friends!* Shaken and confused, he got to his feet. Through the window he saw the first rays of the rising sun.

The room felt cold. He crumpled newspaper and placed it in the hearth, then added kindling and lit a match. When he had a good flame, he added a log. He picked up the quilt and perched on the couch. He sat quietly for a long time, staring at the Christmas Village. He felt overjoyed to be home, but he missed his friends in Canterbury. *But were they even real? Is it possible to miss people who aren't even real?*

Feeling exhausted and confused, Jamie plumped a couch pillow and curled up under the quilt. Something fell out of his shirt. Looking down, he saw a gold medallion dangling from a chain around his neck. He touched it, turning it over in his fingers. It was a St. Jude medallion. St. Jude, the Patron Saint of Lost Causes. Jamie's heart leapt as he touched the good luck charm that his good friend Kelly Pennysworth from Canterbury had given him. He burst into laughter, even as hot tears streamed down his face. *It was real! I knew it! I knew it! I knew it!*

CHAPTER 36

"My goodness, you're up early!" Grandma said. She wore a green gingham check apron with red poinsettias embroidered on the pockets. It was exactly like Ida's apron, and the sight of it almost brought tears to Jamie's eyes as he stood at the door, his arms loaded with firewood. He inhaled the familiar smells of Grandma's kitchen – fresh ground coffee and pecan-cinnamon buns.

"I thought I'd bring in more wood," Jamie said.

Grandma poured herself a cup of steaming coffee and turned on the stove. "Pancakes for breakfast?"

"Sounds good! What can I do to help?"

Grandma peeled off strips of bacon and laid them in a frying pan. "Well this is quite a turnaround from yesterday! What's gotten into you?"

"I dunno," he said, grinning, "I guess it must be the Christmas spirit."

Just then, Grandpa and Mom came into the kitchen. "MOM!" Jamie cried and ran to her. He hugged her for a long time, then pulled away and looked up at her surprised face. "Mom, I'm really sorry for acting so awful. And I'm sorry for all the mean things I've said. Ever."

"Good grief!" Mom cried, pulling him close again and ruffling his hair. "What's gotten into you?"

"That's what I wondered, too," said Grandma, shaking her head. "He says it's the Christmas spirit."

"Grandpa!" Jamie cried and ran to hug him.

"Well, who cares the reason, it's nice to see you smile again," Grandpa said, patting Jamie's back.

All through breakfast, Jamie drank in every word of conversation and beamed at his family like they were Santa Claus, the Easter Bunny and the Tooth Fairy all rolled into one. After having been so afraid that he would never get back home or see his family again, he didn't want to let them out of his sight for even a minute. When they finished breakfast, he helped Grandma with the dishes, wiped down the kitchen table and took out the trash.

Around nine-thirty, Mom stepped into the kitchen from the mud room, dressed in her red parka, black quilted boots and the red mittens with white snowflakes that Grandma had knitted. "It's a beautiful day out there; want to join me for a walk, Jamie?"

Jamie had been helping Grandma polish the good silver for Christmas dinner the next day. "Do you mind, Grandma? I'd like to go."

Grandma smiled and took the polishing rag from his hand. "Go on. We're almost done here anyway."

Jamie bundled up and joined his mother outside. It was cold, but the sun was strong and there was no wind. Fresh, clean Vermont air filled his lungs. The smell of wood smoke from the chimney reminded him of being at Ida's.

Mom said, "Let's head over to the wall across the field. I used to love to balance along that wall when I was small." She lifted her face and let the sun shine on it. She inhaled the cold air deeply into her lungs. "Your Auntie Jess and I had a lot of fun playing in these fields when we were kids."

"I bet," said Jamie. Then he added, "I love it here, too, Mom." Jamie looked up at the clear sky. "I wonder if it will snow. It should have snowed by now."

They trudged along, watching their footing over the uneven ridges and valleys the rain had cut into the earth, which had now frozen hard. After a while, Mom asked, "Are you in the mood to talk?"

"Sure. What do you want to talk about?"

"Well," she said, "we've been through a lot and I know it's been hard on you."

"It's been hard on you too." Jamie looked down at his boots as he trudged along. "I'm sorry I took it all out on you, Mom."

"It's not your fault, Jamie. None of it is. You have every right to be hurt and angry with Dad. It's completely natural. I'm angry with him too," she said, her voice growing tighter. "I could forgive him for what he did – for messing up with the money, but it's hard to forgive him for leaving us. Especially for leaving you. I've had a really hard time forgiving him for that."

"Me too." They reached the wall and Jamie sat down. Mom sat beside him. Grandma and Grandpa's house looked tiny in the distance. "I know what you mean, Mom," Jamie said. "I know that what Dad did with the money was wrong, but we could have gotten over it. It wouldn't have been so bad."

Mom took off her mittens and rested her hands in her lap. She looked up at the sky and seemed to be thinking. She hunched her shoulders up around her neck, then let them sag back down. At last she said, "You know, Jamie, there's a big part of me that still believes there is more to what happened than we know. I still believe Dad is basically a good person. I think that he truly believed it would be better for us if he was gone – that somehow he was protecting us by leaving. I don't think he realized how awful it would make us feel."

Jamie nodded. "I've been so mad at him. Sometimes I just wanted to scream and kick things! But a lot has happened …." Jamie caught himself before blurting out how everything that happened to him in Canterbury had helped him understand what it was like to feel afraid and alone, and how it had helped him see how Dad must have felt when things went wrong.

He started over. "I mean, I've been thinking about it a lot, and I think that for Dad to do what he did, he must have felt really scared. Now it kind of feels like the anger is clogging up my heart and I want it to stop."

"I know exactly what you mean." Mom reached over and took Jamie's hand in hers. "You can't flip forgiveness on like a light switch, so I think it will probably take us a long time to really and truly forgive him. But maybe we should just start with trying not to be so angry anymore. Do you think we could try that?"

Jamie dug the frozen ground with the heel of his boot. Then he looked up and said, "Yes. I'm really tired of being angry. It's exhausting."

She squeezed his hand. "Good. It's a good place to start."

"Do you think he'll come back?"

Mom sighed and looked down. "I really don't know if he will. And that's why you and I have to be able to talk to each other. We have some important decisions to make, and I want us to make them together. I want us to be on the same team from now on."

Jamie thought about how he hadn't let his friends in Canterbury down when it really mattered, even though he had been petrified that staying to help them might mean he could never get back home. "It turns out that I can be a pretty good person to have on a team, Mom. I won't let you down. You can count on me."

She smiled. "Good to know. And I promise that from now on we'll talk about everything, and we'll decide things together. Deal?"

"Deal."

"Okay. So one of the first things we'll have to figure out is if we're going back to Hardcastle. We don't have to decide anything right this minute, but we should decide what we want to do by New Year's."

Jamie said, "At first I thought I wanted us to stay here, but that's because it seemed too hard to go back. Coming here was like being able to escape."

"What do you think now?"

Jamie wrinkled his nose. "Now I think it would be kind of like doing what Dad did. I've figured out that you can't really run away from problems."

Mom looked at him, surprised. "When did my son suddenly become so wise?" She was quiet for moment, then said, "You know, Jamie, we really do have friends in Hardcastle who will stand by us if we decide to go back. And if we go back, I'll call Tommy's parents. Maybe they'll come around. But anyway, you're good at making new friends, right?"

Jamie smiled like he had a secret. "You're right, I am," he said. Then he thought of something else. "Mom, will we have to sell the house?"

"Yes. The money from the sale has to go toward paying back the money owed to Dad's clients. But I make a good living writing for the magazine, and I can freelance too. In the meantime, we can find a nice small house. It wouldn't be so bad, would it?"

"No. It would be okay." Jamie grinned and added, "Or, we could buy an RV and just travel all over the country."

Mom chuckled. "Or, we could join the Peace Corps!"

"Cool! Wait, I'm probably too young for that, right?

"Right." Mom stood up and pulled on her mittens. Gray clouds had gathered overhead while they talked, erasing the blue sky and blocking the sun. A pair of chickadees flew by and landed in the scrubby underbrush. "I love chickadees. They're such little birds, but they stay behind and stick out these cold New England winters while the bigger birds fly south."

Jamie watched as the small birds with their round bodies, black-capped heads and fuzzy white chests picked at the brush. "We could be like the chickadees, Mom."

"On the other hand, there's a difference between 'running away' and 'making a new start.' We can settle down wherever we want to really. So let's keep our options open."

"Okay, Mom. I like that idea."

She looked up at the milky gray sky. "The day is changing. Let's head back."

Trudging beside his mother across the hard brown field, Jamie thought about how much had changed in the short time since they'd come to Bell's Crossing. He'd lived two lives really, in the past four days — one life here and one in Canterbury. He shook his head, still amazed by it all.

"Jamie?" Mom asked, interrupting his thoughts.

"Yeah?"

"I'm glad you're on my team." She giggled like a little kid. "Hey, we could be Team Jamisa!"

"Huh?"

"You know, like a combination of our names — Jamie and Lisa."

"Oh, I get it," Jamie said, laughing. "Or Team Lamie."

Mom said, "Oh — that sounds too much like Lame! We don't want to be the Lame Team!"

"Okay then, how about Team Reynolds?"

"Works for me. I like it." Mom wrapped her arm around Jamie's shoulders and he wrapped his arm around her waist.

Something wet landed on the tip of Jamie's nose. He looked up, expecting to see rain. Instead, he saw a few large snowflakes spinning aimlessly overhead. "Hey, Mom! It's snowing!" For a moment they stood perfectly still in the middle of the field, watching the snowflakes quietly gather in the air around their heads and listening to the silence. Smiling, they started walking again.

As they neared the house, Grandma and Grandpa's front porch came into view. It made Jamie think of the night he'd sat crying on Ida's porch, homesick and afraid that he would never get home or see his mom again. He remembered how Rusty had comforted him, and what he had said to Jamie that night about things working out. Jamie said, "Mom, don't worry, okay? Whatever we decide, things will work out. They always do."

She threw back her head and laughed, a real, true laugh like Jamie hadn't heard from her in a long, long time. "Who are you and what have you done with my son?" she cried. Then she mussed Jamie's thick hair with her red mitten, and he didn't even try to stop her.

CHAPTER 37

"Want to play checkers, Grandpa?" Jamie asked.

Grandpa looked up from his book and raised one thick, bushy white eyebrow. "Sure you wouldn't rather play with some of those video games of yours?"

Jamie grinned. "Nope! I'd rather hang out here with you."

Grandpa shrugged. "Well, okay, then. Bring on the checkers!"

Jamie set the checkerboard on the table in front of the fireplace. Grandpa sat in his leather chair, and Jamie pulled up a ladder-backed chair for himself. Grandma worked her knitting, while Mom lay on the couch reading Jamie's copy of *From Time to Time*. "What time is the tree lighting tonight?" she asked.

"Seven o'clock," answered Grandma. "We'll have an early supper before we go down."

Jamie said, "Grandma, you didn't tell me that Canterbury is a real place."

Grandma looked over her half glasses. "I didn't?"

"No."

"Well, sure it is. It's about fifteen miles from here. My village is supposed to be an exact replica of the town the way it looked in 1932. The whole story is right there on the boxes." Grandma's knitting needles paused in mid-air. "Go get one out of that cupboard and you can read about it for yourself."

Jamie pulled out a cardboard box that had a picture of Ida's Boarding House on one side, and a logo and some printing on the other.

Grandma said, "As I recall, my Christmas Village was made by some family that actually lived in Canterbury back in the thirties. They had a funny name ... Oh! What was it?" She tipped her head back as if it would help her remember. "Something like Moneyspoon. No, that's not it ... Moneysworth?"

"Pennysworth."

Jamie's head whipped around and his jaw dropped open. He stared bug-eyed at his mother.

"Why are you looking at me like that?" Mom asked.

"*PENNYSWORTH?*" Jamie cried, his heart racing. "Are you *sure?*"

"Yes, I'm sure," Mom said. "The village was designed by two sisters and a brother from Canterbury. Their name was Pennysworth. It's all there on the box."

"Two sisters? Are you sure it was two sisters, not just a brother and a sister?"

Mom gave Jamie a puzzled look. "It's been a long time since I read it, but yes, I'm pretty sure. I remember because it was such an interesting story about why they had the village made. Why?"

"Is that where you got those stories you told me on the couch the other night?"

Mom tipped her head, thinking. "I guess it must be."

Jamie's hands shook as he turned over the box. He saw that the logo was a drawing of two hands reaching out to each other. A chill ran up his spine and he began to read aloud:

"In 1932, Kelly Pennysworth was a happy ten year old living in Canterbury, Vermont. It was the Great Depression. Times were tough. Jobs were scarce. But Canterbury was a pretty and peaceful town where people looked out for each other and lent a helping hand.

"Just before Christmas, Kelly fell through the ice while skating with her brother Christopher. She would have drowned were it not for the sudden appearance of a mysterious stranger, a twelve year old boy who seemed to have no memory of who he was or where he came from. In the days after the rescue, the people of Canterbury took the boy under their wing, and he, Kelly and Christopher became the best of friends.

"On Christmas Eve, tragedy nearly struck again when a baby named Emilie was kidnapped and held for ransom. Again, the mysterious young stranger played a pivotal role in saving Emilie and returning her to her loving mother, Iris Gordon, who, coincidentally, worked for the Pennysworth family. That same Christmas Eve, the boy disappeared as mysteriously as he had arrived. Kelly and Christopher never saw him again, but he remained in their memories and in their hearts always.

"A few years later, Mr. Pennysworth, a widower, married Iris Gordon, and Emilie, Kelly and Christopher became brother and sisters. In 1958, Kelly came up with the idea of creating a miniature scene that exactly replicated the town of Canterbury as it looked and felt during that fateful Christmas of 1932."

Jamie looked up. "Grandma, when did you buy the village?" he asked.

She thought for a moment. "I bought it at the Canterbury General Store in 1958. I remember because it was our first Christmas together as a married couple. We had just bought this house – oh, it was such a wreck then!" Grandma sighed, remembering. "Anyway, we didn't have any Christmas decorations and I fell in love with the village instantly. They said there were only a few of them in existence, so I snapped this one up."

Jamie went on reading, the box quivering in his shaky hands. "Only a few villages were made and sold in local Vermont stores. The Pennysworth family dedicated them with great love and gratitude to Jamie, the mysterious boy who saved two lives."

Mom said, "That's where I first heard the name Jamie, when I read about the heroic boy who saved the girl from drowning. I liked the name and always thought that if I had a son, I would name him Jamie."

Jamie's mind reeled. He closed his eyes, allowing the meaning of what he had just read to sink in. It seemed almost impossible to believe, yet he knew without a doubt that what he was thinking now was true.

In 1932, Kelly almost drowns, but is saved by me, a time traveler from 2007. I tell her that I got there through a miniature Christmas Village owned by my grandmother.

In 1958, Kelly and Emilie create the Christmas Village, supposedly to preserve their memory of the town the way it looked when they were young.

Just before Christmas, 1958, my grandmother buys one of the villages. Kelly and Christopher knew that she would buy one, because I told them the village was in her house in 2007.

In 2007, I am magically pulled into the Christmas Village and back in time to Canterbury, 1932, where I save Kelly and help save Emilie.

Jamie opened his eyes. His head was spinning and he felt dizzy. Then he grinned.

"They made the village so that I could come."

"What's that, son?" Grandpa asked.

"Oh nothing, Grandpa." Jamie put the box back in the cupboard. He walked to the table and looked down at the Christmas Village, the place that for the past few days had been like a second home to him. He reached out and touched the tiny skaters. *They believed me, and they made sure that I could come.*

CHAPTER 38

Christmas Eve had been such a strange and wonderful day. Wonderful, because Jamie felt so grateful to be home again with his mother and grandparents. Strange, because of what he had learned about the Christmas Village and its connection with Kelly, Chris and Emilie. Wonderful because he and Mom were on the same team again, and strange, because the intense anger Jamie had felt toward his father seemed to have melted like snowflakes on his tongue.

And it was a strange and bittersweet feeling, standing on the Bell's Crossing common on Christmas Eve, looking at a giant pine tree awash in lights, a crowd of people gathered around the bonfire, singing carols. A dusting of snow now covered the ground, and flakes continued to drift lazily down. At times Jamie felt confused about where he was. Just last night he had been standing with Kelly and Christopher on the Canterbury common on Christmas Eve, gazing at a giant pine tree awash in lights, a bonfire blazing and the crowd singing carols.

The wood smoke from the fire smelled familiar and comforting. The sounds of laughter and singing melted together like hot fudge sauce on ice cream. Jamie gazed up at the full moon, now blurred behind hazy clouds. Just last night he had gazed at the moon from a different place and time.

As homesick as he had been for his family, Jamie now felt just as homesick for the friends he left behind in Canterbury, friends that he knew he would never see again. He constantly had the feeling that he might turn around and see them at any moment.

Suddenly Jamie glimpsed a girl with long golden braids, wearing a bright red coat and a Santa's hat. She was standing near the bonfire with her back to him. His heart lurched. *Kelly!* The crowd shifted and the girl disappeared from sight. Jamie raced across the common. *There she is!* Jamie ran up behind the girl and tapped her on the shoulder. "Kelly?"

She turned around. She looked like Kelly, with her fair skin, golden braids and almond-shaped blue eyes. But it wasn't Kelly.

"Hi! No, my name isn't Kelly. It's Kendall. Kendall Wainwright."

"I ... I'm sorry," Jamie stammered. "You look a lot like someone I know."

The girl smiled. "What's your name?"

Jamie answered, "I'm Jamie Reynolds."

Kendall broke into a wide grin. "Your name is Jamie Reynolds?"

"Yes," he answered, wrinkling his brow. "Why?"

"Wait! Right! Here!" Kendall ordered. Jamie smiled, thinking that she reminded him of Kelly in more ways than one. He watched as she ran over to a white-haired woman who stood on the far side of the bonfire. The old woman bent forward to talk with Kendall, and then turned to talk to a gray-haired woman standing nearby. The women linked arms and Kendall marched them over to where Jamie stood, hands in pockets, looking and feeling very confused.

"Grandma," Kendall said, "I'd like you to meet Jamie." Kendall grinned at Jamie and arched her brows. She looked downright gleeful, as though she had a big secret that she could barely stand to keep to herself another second.

"And Jamie, I'd like you to meet my grandmother."

The white-haired woman smiled. She had deep lines and creases around her eyes and mouth, but her skin looked soft and her blue eyes bright. She spoke softly, with a wistful tone in her voice. "I've been waiting a very long time for this night."

"Why?" Jamie asked.

"A long, long time ago, when I was a little girl, a young boy saved my life. He said that he lived in Bell's Crossing and came from the future."

Jamie's eyes flew wide. A shiver ran up his spine.

"I believed him, and so I knew that he would be in Bell's Crossing tonight, Christmas Eve, 2007. I just hoped that he would come to the tree lighting ceremony so that I could find him. I've been waiting a long time to see him again."

Tears streamed down the woman's face. Jamie felt hot tears on his own cheeks. The woman opened her arms and he ran into them. They held each other for a long time.

Kendall said, "Let me do a proper introduction. Grandma, this is Jamie Reynolds. And Jamie, this is my grandmother, Kelly Pennysworth Wainwright."

Jamie nodded, wiping his eyes. "And this," Kendall said, indicating the gray-haired woman, "Is my great-aunt Emilie."

"Hello, Jamie. I was just a baby when you saved me, so I never got a chance to thank you. I'd like to thank you now," Emilie said. She smiled, her brown eyes twinkling and a deep dimple creasing her left cheek.

"You're welcome," Jamie whispered. He could scarcely speak. "This is so incredible! I just saw you yesterday and you were ...."

"Young?" Kelly asked, smiling.

Jamie nodded. "I'm sorry, that probably seemed rude."

She shook her head. "No, Jamie, it's just life. I'm sure this must be very strange for you. After all, for you it was just yesterday that you saw me, and I was only ten years old and Emilie was just a baby. But for us, it's been a whole lifetime — seventy-five years. We've had a long, long time to think about this moment."

"Is Chris here?" Jamie asked.

Kelly shook her head. "No, I'm sorry. He's gone now. But he lived a good long life. You remember what a great story-teller he was?"

Jamie nodded. "He sure was! The best!"

"Well, Chris became a writer. A pretty famous one actually. He wrote fantasy and science fiction books using the pen name C. P. Franklin."

"C.P. Franklin! I love his books! I just finished reading *From Time to Time*."

Kelly smiled and said, "I know. You told us."

Jamie nodded again, remembering. "I guess I gave him the title for his book." Then a wave of sadness hit him. "I'm sorry about Chris," he said, his voice breaking. "He was a true friend."

"He was a good brother too." Kelly was quiet for a moment. Then her face brightened. "But he did make it to see the Sox win the Series in 2004. He was so excited – like a kid in a candy store. He kept saying, 'Jamie was right – it was a very, very, very, *very* long wait!'"

Jamie grinned. "I'm glad he got to see that. What ever happened to Jim? And Ida and Rusty and all the guys? And Reggie?" He wanted to know everything.

Kelly said, "They fished Jim out of the pond and he went to jail for a long time. After a while my father and Iris realized they were in love, something we kids had figured out long before they did! They got married and Emilie became our sister. Ida and Rusty got married too, and years later turned the boarding house into a four-star Bed and Breakfast Inn. I don't know what happened to all the men – some of them left town. But Big Ed and Little Ed stayed and eventually bought the hardware store together.

"When the Second World War started, Vanderzee's reopened and was busier than ever. Oh! And here's the best part! Reggie became a local hero. The dentist gave him new teeth for free, and later he ran for mayor and won! In fact, he was our mayor for more than thirty years, and a darn good one too."

Jamie shook his head, amazed at the wonder of all that had happened. "I know about the Christmas Village," he said.

Kelly and Emilie exchanged knowing smiles. Emilie said, "When it got to be the late 1950's and we still hadn't seen anything like the village you described, Kelly realized that we could have it made ourselves. She was so proud of herself when she thought of it, but then we felt silly for not thinking of it sooner. It seemed so obvious that we were supposed to do it."

Jamie asked, "But how did you know it would work?"

Emilie shrugged. "We knew it would work, because you had already come."

"Do you know *how* it works?"

"We have no idea!" Kelly said, laughing. "We've been hoping that maybe you've been able to figure it out."

Jamie shook his head. "I have absolutely no idea either."

Kendall said, "Well then, I guess it must be magic!"

"That's right!" they all said at once, and burst into laughter.

Jamie asked, "Would you like to come over to our house? I don't know how we'll explain how we know each other, but I'd like you to meet my mom and my grandparents."

"We'll just tell them the truth," said Kelly. "We'll tell them that we just met, but we became instant friends."

CHAPTER 38

"That will work," Jamie said, smiling.

"And Jamie?" Kelly grinned mischievously, her blues eyes sparkling.

"Yes?"

"Maybe we can play checkers. I've had a lot of time to practice!"

AUTHOR'S NOTE

It wasn't until 1937, when Disney released the movie, *Snow White and the Seven Dwarfs,* that the dwarves became known as Doc, Grumpy, Happy, Sleepy, Bashful, Sneezy and Dopey. But because these names are so ingrained in our popular culture, I have asked the reader to indulge me in a minor historical discrepancy, for the sake of our story and a chuckle.

Made in the USA
Charleston, SC
27 October 2013